FAIRY TALES UNRAVELLED

ONCE UPON A TIME... IT ALL BECAME DEADLY!

ALANA GREIG

Cover design MARMADUKE THE SPY

Edited by BRITNEY ANDEWS

Formatting by CRESCENT MOON

CRAZY INK

CRAZY INK

FAIRY TALE UNRAVELLED BY ALANA GREIG

PUBLISHED BY CRAZY INK

COVER DESIGN © MARMADUKE THE SPY PRODUCTIONS

EDITING BY BRITTNEY ANDREWS

FORMATTING BY CRESCENT MOON DESIGN

ACKNOWLEDGMENTS

THANK YOU TO MARMADUKE THE SPY PRODUCTIONS FOR THE COVER. I KNOW WE HAD SOME DO OVERS, BUT I KNEW WE WOULD GET THERE.

TO EVERYONE WHO THOUGHT ABOUT GIVING UP ON THEIR DREAMS.
DON'T, YOU ARE STRONGER THAN YOU KNOW.
NEVER LET THAT MAGIC INSIDE YOU DIE. THE WORLD NEEDS DREAMERS LIKE YOU.

FOREWORD

This is a book that never should have been. It is a combination of previously published work and brand-new stories.

There is something evocative about fairy tales and I just didn't feel like I had scratched the itch with this idea.

This is a collection of my twisted imagination and the classic fairytales that gave me inspiration. Twenty-four retells of some well-known and some you may never have heard of fairy tales that you shouldn't read to your children at bedtime. I really explored levels of intensity with these short stories. Some are quite tame while others have caused quite a reaction. My husband read some, and one in particular had him turn to me and say, "You are really messed up."

I took that as a compliment. As an author it is my goal to get a reaction from my readers. It isn't always going to be a great reaction; that is the risk of putting yourself out there. The written word has always been a huge love of mine and love this or loath it, thank you for taking a chance and purchasing this collection.

One last thing, I am a British author, therefore these tales are written using standard English. I have included a glossary of the more unusual words in the book.

Enjoy your tumble down the rabbit hole of unraveled reality. Try not to get too caught up in the madness.

Alana

GLOSSARY OF ENGLISH TERMS

Caul
The amniotic membrane enclosing a foetus.

Folly
A costly ornamental building with no practical purpose, especially a tower or mock-Gothic ruin built in a large garden or park.

Verge
A grass edging such as that by the side of a road or path.

Puce
A dark red or purple-brown colour.

Put paid to
Stop abruptly; destroy.

By the name of
Called.

Rubbed along

Cope or manage without undue difficulty.

Pyjamas

Night wear, top and bottoms.

Mould

A hollow container used to give shape to molten or hot liquid material when it cools and hardens.

Entrails

A person's or animal's intestines or internal organs, especially when removed or exposed.

Hilt

The handle of a weapon or tool, especially a sword, dagger, or knife.

Squire

A young nobleman acting as an attendant to a knight before becoming a knight himself.

Tell tale

A person, especially a child, who reports others' wrongdoings or reveals their secrets.

Sans

Middle English: from Old French sanz, from a variant of Latin sine 'without'.

Bairn

A child.

Bonny

Attractive or beautiful.

Wendy House

A play house for children .Term originates from Wendy's House in Peter Pan.

DEAREST READER, PLEASE TAKE CARE, THE WORLD GOES TOPSY TURVY FROM HERE.
THE STORIES YOU LOVED AT YOUR MOTHER'S KNEE, HAVE BEEN TWISTED AND CORRUPTED AS YOU WILL SEE.
PLEASE HAVE A CARE WHEN TURNING THESE PAGES, THAT THOSE SMALLER EARS DON'T HEAR THESE
STORIES.
IF YOU STILL DESIRE TO TURN THE NEXT PAGE AND DISCOVER THE WORLD WHERE NIGHTMARES AND UNCOMFORTABLE TRUTHS REIN. THEN TAKE A BREATH
AND GO ON IN, IT'S ALL THERE WAITING TO TICKLE YOUR BRAIN.
WITH ALL THAT SAID LET US BE CLEAR, IT IS ONLY A STORY BOOK, THERE IS NOTHING REAL TO FEAR.
SO, LET US BEGIN, ARE YOU READY?

ONCE UPON A TIME, IT ALL BECAME DEADLY!

IT'S TIME TO TUMBLE DOWN THE RABBIT HOLE AND DESCEND INTO THE MADNESS

RABBIT HOLE

BASED ON ALICE IN WONDERLAND

Alice was in Wonderland . It was a day like any other the pansies were singing, and Cheshire cat was appearing and disappearing in time with the beat. The tiger lilies purred and dropped pollen in her hair. It wasn't perfect, but she couldn't be happier. It was the same dream she had every night. It was the one about being back with her friends in the most magical place she could possibly imagine.

So, the day the White Rabbit appeared in her Surrey back garden came as a bit of a shock. Alice, now twenty-three and a university student of philosophy, was more logical these days. She knew by now, that Wonderland had been a product of her imagination and a place she could only visit in her sleep. Long ago, she'd written it all off as a brilliant daydream that swept her up in her girlhood and kept her safe and content though those summer-filled years. Or so she thought.

Due to this belief, the sight of the rabbit came as quite a surprise. Her glass of milk slipped from her manicured hand and hit the tile floor, creating a loud smashing sound.

But she didn't notice. Alice had bigger problems. In this moment, she needed to see the rabbit up close. Because it *couldn't* be the same rabbit. That was impossible. She was a woman grown, with a partner and a life.

Jill. What would she think? Jill would think she had lost the plot. They had been together two years, but even Alice knew her girlfriend was not ready to take on a crazy person of this particular kind. There was only so much a relationship could take.

Still, she opened the back door and walked down to the garden in her sweatpants and vest top. It was a chilly morning; the breeze whipped her newly dyed pink hair across her eyes. When she was able to see again, she noticed the rabbit was still sitting exactly where she had seen him from the house.

"Hello Mr. Rabbit, are you lost?"

No, but you're mental.

Was she really addressing a rabbit at eight o'clock on a Tuesday morning in her pyjamas? The rabbit did not answer, which was expected. It was, she reminded herself, a rabbit after all. She wanted to work out *why* it was just sitting there. As a rule, these animals are scared of everything. It should have run off the moment it saw her or when it caught the scent of her cat.

Still it did not move.

"Well, good morning; I now have to go and clean my kitchen thanks to you."

Without looking back, Alice returned to her house and carried on with her day.

That night, the dreams started right back up. Back in Wonderland, the gardens were afire with blue flames. The smoke billowed into a violent orange sky. Screams filled the air, and the smell caught in her throat. Alice knew she was in Wonderland once more. But this was *not* the place of her childhood. This was a place twisted and broken.

She should wake up, then the screams would be no more, and Jill would be next to her, snoring in that cute way she had always snored—two snorts, one pause, two snorts again. Jill was consistent.

Alice, not so much. But at least she was lucky. Usually, she could control her dreams to a degree. If she did not like them, she could wake herself up. She never told anyone this, not even Jill. It was her special thing. Tonight though, this trick was not working. Alice was stuck in the wasteland that had once been her favourite place.

Deciding to explore, Alice made her way through the garden of giant flowers and headed to the Mad Hatter's house. What she found on her arrival was beyond description. Piles of body parts were stacked on the chairs of his beloved tea table. Bloated flies and maggots were feasting on the soft tissues that were still glistening with moisture.

She let out a sob when she spied Hatter's hat atop his broken body at the head of the table, blood dripping from its purple brim. She could not stay here, not with the birds that would be next to pick out dead eyes and gorge on bulging intestines, now that she'd opened the door and let the death smell permeate outside.

Instead, she ran. It was some time before Alice stopped running. The mantra of "wake up, wake the fuck up" was as rhythmic as Jill's snoring, but equally useless. Alice was trapped here, and unless she found a way to wake up, *this* would be her new reality.

"ALICE, ALICE, wake up. You just kicked me out of the bed, you crazy bitch."

Jill staggered to her feet; the fall from their overly high bed onto the hardwood floor was not the wake-up she wanted. Frankly, she never wanted any kind of wake- up at three-thirty in the morning. Stumbling over to her thrashing girlfriend, Jill gripped her by her shoulders and shook her.

"Wake. The. Hell. Up." Nothing.

She tried holding her nose closed, running her knuckles along Alice's sternum, and more, but still nothing woke her. The thrashing had stopped, but Alice was out, and a cold sweat had bloomed over her pale skin.

Jill was a tough one who wasn't known for giving up easily. She was a couple of years older than Alice and worked as a correction officer at the local prison. She had seen it all and then some. Nothing scared her. But the sight of her Alice in bed terrified her. She fell to her knees, praying for someone—anyone—to help her.

ALICE FELL HARD to her knees. Someone had pushed her. The same unseen assailant now threw her onto her back, only to rise her up and throw her down again and again. Excruciating pain shot through her skull. Whoever, or whatever *"it"* was, wanted her dead. She tried to get up, but found that now she was somehow pinned to the floor. Water mixed with bodily fluids was rising around her inert form. It was at that very moment that Alice knew she was going to die.

Jill was at a loss. She knelt by the bed trying to figure out what to do next. Finally, she stood back up to assess the situation again: Alice had all the signs of drowning; she knew this because Google was a great tool, and she had seen someone drown once. It was a sight she could never forget, and it was all she could think of. Like back then, brown-tinged, rancid water flowed from Alice's mouth. The smell was horrific; it was as if the room was filled with decaying flesh and excrement. It was the kind of smell that one can taste. Jill gagged. She needed air. But she didn't have time. Sick to her stomach, she started chest compressions on her girlfriend. She had no clue what the fuck was going on. But there was no way Alice was dying today. *Come back to me!* It was no use. After twenty minutes of working on her, she ran to get the phone.

The bed was soaked in slimy fluids by the time Jill got back to Alice. She had only crossed the room and back. There was already a puddle on the floor and the comforter was saturated in a tan layer of bile. She had flashbacks of watching horror movies and the drowning she'd never spoken of.

But this was different, almost like a possession. Was that what was happening to her girl? Was she possessed? Jill was an atheist, as was Alice. No religion that told them their love was wrong was worth their time. But right now, she was willing to pray again to any and all higher powers if it meant Alice would live through this night. Climbing back onto the bed, Jill straddled her lover and restarted the lifesaving compressions that would hopefully expel the water from her lungs. The phone was forgotten. It was all on her to save Alice's life.

BACK IN WONDERLAND, filthy water covered Alice. Her last-hope breath before she was submerged was almost spent. Alice knew that this would be one of the most painful ways to die. Her chest burned with the need to breathe; she would soon have no choice, even though it would be the death of her. As reflex took over and the primal need to survive that is hardwired in every human being kicked in, the putrid water rushed into Alice's open mouth, filling her lungs, choking her. She convulsed. In the water poured, her lungs trying to expel the fluid but on every retching exhale there was a reflexive inhale. Every muscle in her body screamed. She wanted to free herself. The attack left her weak, and her head hurt so much.

My fight to survive this is strong. It became her mantra, and she repeated it over and over again.

She fought the weight of the water as her vision began to cloud. Her chest hurt so much, but she needed to hold on, just a little longer. If she could sit up, she told herself, she had a chance. Her arms burned with the effort. They did not move, but still she tried. Just as she was moments from death, she felt a great pressure on her chest.

This is it, the moment I die. Her mantra was gone.

She wanted to scream; every rib in her chest was bowing and popping. The being was back and was crushing her chest, hastening her death. The pressure forced the water out of her lungs, but it was all in vain. For every agonising compression and the violent expulsion of fluid, there was another rapid intake of the liquid that was killing her.

I love you, Jill.

THE COMPRESSIONS WERE USELESS. Jill knew it. She knew that Alice was dead, but she just couldn't stop.

Where had the water come from? How can someone spew a lake of shit-filled water and be asleep in bed? What the fuck just happened?

A cry ripped its way through Jill and echoed throughout their home. They had plans. The adoption was only finalised yesterday. Tomorrow they were painting the nursery in anticipation of the arrival of their own little girl. Now, everything was ruined. Alice was dead, and Jill didn't know how to carry on.

The police needed to be called, she knew that. She would be taken in for questioning for sure. If that happened, she might lose little Diana. There was no way she could lose both her girls in the same night. She needed to get rid of the body. Burn it, bury it, whatever. There was no way anyone could know that Alice was dead. Looking down at the girl she loved more than anything, Jill kissed her cold, wet mouth. The water had stopped. The taste of the filth made Jill gag again, but she had to kiss her goodbye. In that moment, she felt she had no other choice. She had tried to save her, but this was something beyond the ordinary, and it would take extraordinary measures to patch it up even a little.

Rolling the body in the sodden comforter, Jill was suddenly thankful that they had not started work on the garage yet. The floor had been removed and only bare earth remained. There was a connecting door in the hall, so she would not be seen. She checked the clock, her mind racing, as the adrenaline took over. *4:15.* She had time. Throwing the petite Alice over her shoulder, Jill made her way slowly to the garage.

. . .

IT WAS FREEZING OUT THERE; a situation not helped by her bare feet sinking into the damp mud.

I can't believe I am about to bury my girlfriend within the foundation of my fucking garage. I need a drink.

Jill started to place Alice down as gently as she could, but the body slipped out of her hands at the last moment. The sickening sound of her skull hitting the pile of broken concrete that was once the floor made Jill throw up. Wiping her mouth with her sleeve, Jill went back into the house and returned with a shovel and a bottle of vodka.

The digging took hours, and the vodka was half gone by the time Jill was satisfied the hole was deep enough that no one would ever find Alice. Climbing out, she moved slowly toward the body. She tried to tell herself it was no longer Alice. Alice was dead and this was just a body. She repeated this in her mind as she pushed it over the lip of the pit. The sound was muted, but it was deathly quiet out, and Jill held her breath, praying that the sound had not carried and woken the neighbours.

"I am so sorry, baby girl. I will love you forever, but I have to do this. Diana needs me and I need her." Jill bit back the sob and reached for her shovel.

THREE YEARS LATER...

JILL AND DIANA only remained in that house for a year, and once she was sure that all suspicion had passed, they moved. She missed Alice every day. She had not killed her, far from it. However, the fact that she had buried her in an unmarked grave made her a criminal. By now, Diana had grown into a precious three-year-old. She loved to be outside in the garden. The Devon air seemed to agree with them both, and their days were filled with music and laughter.

It was on the last day of summer that Diana told her mother that she had seen a white rabbit in the garden. Jill had told her wild rabbits were all over the fields behind their cottage home, and it was most likely looking for a vegetable patch now that the fields were on their fallow year. Diana was insistent that this was a very special rabbit. He wore a funny jacket without arms and had a clock on a string.

Jill was transported back, five years to the night Alice had told her of her dream world, Wonderland, and the way she had found it by following a white rabbit in a waist coat and carrying a pocket watch.

"Maybe it wants to show the way to Wonderland, honey," Jill said, swinging her daughter up into her arms.

"I had a friend once who told me that when she was a girl, she visited Wonderland all the time, and it was always a white rabbit that led the way. Just like the one you saw today."

Diana's eyes were round.

"Do you really think so, Mummy?"

"Why not, sweetheart? If you can dream it, then it can become real."

The words tasted of ash on her tongue. *If you can dream it, then it can become real. Was that what had happened to Alice?* She remembered the night she died. She knew Alice had been having a nightmare. *What if?*

"Mummy, come and play now, we might find the rabbit and our way to Wonderland."

Jill held her daughter close. The fields seemed too quiet now and the woods in the distance a little too dark.

"Come on, little one, let's go inside and make some cookies."

Once safely in the house with little Diana watching a movie and the smell of freshly baked cookies filling the cottage with a sweet, comforting aroma, Jill began to think she had overreacted.

It was while she was at the sink rinsing the plates for the dishwasher the next day that she saw the white rabbit. It was on its hind legs with a watch in hand. It seemed to look her right in the eye and then very deliberately tap the face of its watch with its paw.

"Time was running out," it seemed to tell her. She blinked and the rabbit was gone. But deep down she knew what she had seen, and she also knew it would be back.

Back for her Diana.

ANGEL FACED DEMON

BASED ON BEAUTY AND THE BEAST

I was born on a cold November night. It was a difficult birthing; I was told my mother had laboured for three solid days and nights before I was forced into the world. They say there was much screaming and the midwife collapsed at the mere sight of me.

"That is no child of mine!" my father apparently roared at my exhausted mother, as he slapped her clean across the face. To be as I am and to hear that one's birth caused such violent reactions within the household was not the best day. Though, it was expected. Who would have been pleased to be presented with a twisted parody of humanity?

"He is yours, and I shall love him."

My mother's last words. Even now they mean so much to me; she died a few hours after my birth. The official story was blood loss, but in the 21st century that seems very unlikely to me. I believe my father killed her while she rested. Money can buy you anything, even an alibi. I often wonder why he didn't just have me murdered along with her. There was ample opportunity, he was lord of a great manor, a powerful man. History has proven that those in nobility have often murdered those born deformed. The British are not above that, as much as they wish to believe it so. Yet I lived and was given the education a lordling such as myself should receive. Of course, this was all done covertly; I was given a suite of rooms and my own staff from the day I was born, and that is where I have remained for twenty-seven years, three days and 14 hours to be exact.

Father is still alive; I hear him strolling in the gardens with his dogs, Arthur and Bastion. Giant wolfhounds. Sometimes I sit at my window and watch the two beasts run like the wind across the manicured gardens, towards the giant Douglas pine tree that stands proud at the centre of the walled garden my mother had so loved. I could visit the gardens once a day after dark, unless father was entertaining, then I would miss that day.

I don't know if father acknowledges my existence in the outside world. He never remarried and so there are no other children. Just me, his twisted beast boy. Alexander. I am quite hideous, it is true. I have webbed fingers and toes, severe scoliosis, and my left hand is quite useless. I stand at six feet tall despite my deformed spine. I have dark brown hair and green eyes, like my mother before me. The staff whisper about poor "Alexander the Angel Faced Demon." I hate that they pity me.

I could have had surgeries to correct my spine and had the webbing between my phalanges cut away; I would have gone through many surgeries, taken the pain and been grateful. If only to stop the staff calling me "the angel faced demon." Father, such was his shame, would not allow me to attend even a private institution in another country.

"What if someone were to see you?" he would bluster when I broached the subject at age twelve.

"But, Father, I hurt. I have been reading; there are operations that could really ease the pain and make me more like you." I should have never uttered those words. I will never forget the look in his eyes the moment the words tumbled out of my preadolescent mouth. He was horrified. I knew then that he hated me more than I thought possible. I also learned that he was the true beast within the walls of Hollowed Manor. What kind of parent could leave a child in pain when they had the power to ease it? To this day I have never understood it. I doubt I ever will.

One day I will be free of him and this set of rooms on the second floor. My gilded prison. There is so much I want to see and experience. To fall in love and meet the man of my dreams. Oh yes, that is another thing that my father loathes about me. I am gay. It's laughable really, in this day and age to feel disgusted because a human loves someone of the same gender. I am as God made me, and I will one day find the man I am meant to be with.

That opportunity came ten years later. The Lord Graham Hollowed of Hollowed Manor had passed away in his sleep at the age of fifty-six. I mourned him of course, a beast he may have been, but he did keep me in comfort and provided me with an education. I did not love him, that is true, how can you love someone who you never really knew?

The day of the funeral I was of course unable to attend. That had been some of his last words, "Keep the freak away from my funeral", charming really. The reading of the will was conducted in the drawing room. I again was not invited, and truthfully, I had no interest in hearing the lands and fortune being divided amongst distant family members who, up until he died, had not given my father a second thought. Death really brings out the worst in people. It came as a great surprise to discover that father had left me as his heir. I was the new lord of Hollowed Manor. A shock I am sure, to the room full of my extended family who had never set eyes on me. I did laugh when I was told. I know that was in bad taste. However, the man hated me with a passion yet here I am the lord of all that was his.

Did I want it? That was the question. This house and its lands had been all I had known. The world is a vast place, and I had dreams to explore it and experience everything I could. At almost thirty-eight I have realised that I would likely never meet the man I dreamed of. I cried then, for it all. My birth, my mother, and even my father. He was of a generation that couldn't deal with differences, and he was in a position, that to him, stressed the value of perfection above everything. It was a bitter pill to swallow.

Three days after the reading of the will and my appointment as the new Lord of the Manor, I received a letter, my first ever. It was addressed to The Right Honourable Lord Alexander Hollowed. That took me aback. It all felt very real for the first time. I had arrived.

Enclosed were letters from both my father and my mother. As I sat in my father's old study, drinking Lady Grey tea with my own hound, Grayson, at my feet, I read the letter from my father first.

DEAR ALEXANDER,

The day you were born I was full of such hope for the future of our house. So, you see when I saw you for the first time it was like having the world I had planned so carefully for us snatched away. It was all so cruel. Kathleen, your mother, was so in love with you, her angel baby, the one she thought she would never have. I wanted to snatch you away and smother you. How could you be this when your mother and I were so strong and healthy? I was such a stupid man back then.

I know you believe I had your mother killed; the staff whisper of it in the corridors. My son, you will learn this when you are Lord over them all. No, I will not disinherit you, Alexander. I have been a cruel father and for that I am sorry. There is no reason for what I did other than my pride was badly wounded, and I took it out on you. I believed for the longest time that you were something, someone, to be ashamed of, to hide away and forget about. After your mother died, I was a broken man. She was the light in my life, Alexander. She died in her sleep, a clot in her lungs. Of course, I blamed you for it. How stupid it all seems now knowing that my time is far shorter than I had anticipated.

Maybe it is God's punishment to take me in my prime, for ignoring my only son, my only connection to my Kathleen? I'll find out when I meet my maker, I am sure. If I find your mother in heaven, if I am permitted entry, I will beg at her feet for forgiveness.

So, my son, first and only born of me. I love you. Deep down I always have. Love and hate are separated by a knife-edge. One I have balanced on your whole life. I am sorry I never told you. I am sorry that I wasn't the father you deserved, the one you needed. You have surprised me at every turn; you are handsome and extremely well read. Your school masters have told me over the years that you are nothing short of a genius. I missed it all. I heard you singing once. Your window was open, and I was out in the garden with the dogs. I am not ashamed to say I wept at hearing you. I had never heard such beauty since your mother. You have some many gifts, Alexander, use them my son. Go out into the world and use them.

All my love,

Papa

. . .

I WILL BE HONEST, I was inconsolable for a good few hours after reading his letter. He loved me. After years, decades of near solitude. I couldn't wrap my head around it. I still can't to this day. My mother's letter, I remember not wanting to open it, unsure I could take any more heartache that day or indeed in my lifetime. Taking a breath, I steeled myself and broke the seal on the letter from a woman I had loved my whole life but never met.

My dearest Alexander, my angel,

I knew you would be beautiful, how could you not be? You were created from love. The day you were born I was so tired. You made me wait, my angel, to meet you. Three days of labour were worth it though. How I loved you. Your beauty captivated me the second you were placed in my arms. Your father was emotional too. I don't blame him for what happened in the birthing room; he was taken by surprise. Understand that he had been waiting for your arrival just as much as I. We were told we would never have a child, so to wait for you for nine long months and to have you not be as he expected his son to be was hard on him.

He will get over his shock and see what I see. Our perfect child who we prayed for and now have. I have such plans for us, dear one, but I fear we may not get to see them through. I believe our time is far shorter than it should be. You are brand new and you need me. My body, I fear has other ideas, I can feel there is something wrong. I can't tell your father; he has been through so much already and so I tell you, my angel. Love him, Alex, even if he finds it hard to love you in return. Love him as I love you, with an open heart and an endless supply of compassion and understanding. Family is the most important thing in the world. Remember that and you will always be a rich man.

I am sorry our time is shorter than I had dreamed. You are the thing I am most proud of. You hold my heart forevermore.

. . .

All my love, Mama

So, beauty gave birth to the beast, or so everyone in Hollowed Manor believed. The truth was that beauty married for love, and when her child was born, the shock of his disfigurements turned his father into a beast. But in the end, love won out and the beast turned back into the man.

I never liked fairy tales as a child, I found them dull and impossible. I wonder now though if that is truly the case? True, my story has a touch of the impossible about it. Impossibility is what drives us on though isn't it? To overcome it and succeed no matter the odds.

THREE YEARS LATER....

"Do you, Alexander, take Jonathan to be your life partner?"

The wedding I thought I'd never have, was perfect. At almost forty-two I had received surgery to correct my spine, not for vanity but to ease my pain. Jonathan and I have been very happy together these last two years, and our wedding was all I could have hoped for. My next plan is to adopt some children to fill the manor with laughter and sticky handprints. It's a shame I may never see it. I have cancer, it was found during my back surgery. Stage three bone cancer of the spine. I haven't told Jonathan yet; he is far too happy, and I don't want to steal that joy away from him. I'll write to him like my parents wrote to me. He will have a keepsake then and something to show our children as I have a feeling the paperwork will be accepted in time for us to enjoy a few months of being called Papa together. I wish I could save him and them from what is to come.

His fairy tale is about to become a horror story. Not all horror stories are about murders and ghosts; real horror resides within us all and on occasion it breaks forth and terrifies even those with the strongest of characters. There will be no happy ever after for me. I am the Angel Faced Demon, I shouldn't have expected one.

RICHER THAN LOVE

BASED ON THE GIANT AND THREE GOLDEN HAIRS

One bright summer's morning, a child was born. This child was special. He was born within his caul. His mother was overjoyed as such a birth prophesied long-life, riches, and marriage to a high-born lady.

"My sweet boy, I shall call you William. It is a noble name and will suit you well when you are a lord," Martha spoke the soft words to baby William with hope in her heart that he would have the future she would never be able to offer him.

A few weeks later, while Martha was tending to the chickens and William was laying in his crib in the shade of the old oak tree, a herald approached them. His livery and grey gelding told Martha this was a royal herald. Stumbling to her feet and brushing chicken feed from her callused palms, she approached the little wooden gate to her modest home and waited for the herald to reach her. The sun glinted off his steed's polished tack, causing Martha to shield her eyes from the glinting bridle.

. . .

By the grace of God, what a hovel, the herald thought, casting his small grey eyes over the dwelling and the scruffy peasant before him. "I come in the name of King David. Word has reached the castle that a boy was born with a great prophecy attached to him. Do you know of this boy?"

Martha had no love for the new king. He was a cruel man. In fact, she felt sorry for his wife. She had not been seen since she birthed a daughter last winter. The king had wanted sons; he had not attended the naming ceremony for his own daughter, and that had horrified Martha. Knowing that William could not been seen, she prayed he stay quiet. "Good day, royal herald to our great and kind king, I have heard the murmurs, but alas, my baby died not long after his birth. It pains me so to have lost both him and his father in the same season." Martha willed her eyes to tear.

Sneering at the pathetic creature before him, the herald rolled his eyes. "Very well, I shall leave you to go about your business." With that, he kicked his horse and trotted away, leaving Martha coughing on dust from the road.

I must hide William.

Now that she had lied to a representative of the royal house, she could not keep him here. The thought of being parted from the beloved child broke her tired heart, but she knew that to keep him alive, she must let him go.

William was moved from one family to another, until one winter's night the king's guard came for him. A greedy merchant had given up his whereabouts for two bolts of silk. Six-month-old William was taken to the king at his hunting lodge; he did not want his queen to see the babe in case she fell in love with him. The thought had crossed his mind that he could take the boy home as his ward to keep him from marrying his daughter.

King David was a pragmatic man and did not hold to fairy tales and happy ever afters. His own wife seemed to be unable to bear him a son. The prophecy was likely an old wives' tale to make lower-ranking expectant mothers feel better when the reality was that they would always be poor with no hope of making a good match for their offspring. And yet, he pursued the boy across his kingdom. Not wanting to look too closely at his motives, he looked down at the boy. He was a strong boy with a shock of black hair and startling green eyes.

It's like he can see into my soul.

Turning from the child, he remembered staring into another set of green eyes . . . no, he would not think of that.

"Hector!"

His most trusted knight appeared at his side. "Yes, my king?" Hector was an honourable man; this kidnapping did not sit well with him. With his back to the Moses basket, the king ordered that he take the squalling brat and dump him in the river. He felt sick but did not show his distaste to the king. Picking up the basket, Sir Hector left the room.

The journey to the water's edge was not far as the river was swollen from the last rain and the current was fast. Looking at the young boy, he thought of the child's mother and the waste of an innocent life over a superstition. Checking that no one was watching, he carried on along the river until he came upon some fisher wives. They glared at him as they wished him good day.

If the king finds out, I shall be hanged from the battlements!

Searching the faces of the women, he found what he was looking for green eyes. He approached the woman and her eyes never left his. *This one will protect him.* Hector dropped to his knees before her.

"This babe needs a home. I will give you five gold coins to take him with you. His name is John. Keep him hidden. Will you do this for me?"

The woman looked into the eyes of Sir Hector; everyone knew who he was. Sophie wanted to refuse the child. If this was his bastard, he should raise him. It was then she looked at the child as he began to fuss in his basket. In that moment, she fell in love.

"Yes, I shall take the child, I have none of my own and no husband to speak of, but that is no matter to my people," she replied, already reaching into the basket to pick up the child who would henceforth call her Mother.

Relief washed over Hector. Reaching for his purse, he gave her the whole thing. It would buy her passage that would take them far from here.

"Take it all and leave this land. I beg of you."

Eyes wide, Sophie took the purse and hid it in the folds of her skirt. Laying the baby back in his blankets and taking her by the elbow, Hector walked with her to the king's road and waited for a merchant to pass by. The day was fine, but he knew the chill would be brought with the dusk. Helping her into the back of a wine merchant's trailer, she and the babe snuggled amongst the barrels of wine and crates of salted meats. He bid her and the child farewell.

I pray the king never hears of this day.

TWENTY YEARS LATER...

. . .

"MA . . . MAAAAAA! I'm going now. I will be back tomorrow . . . Ma?" John knew she couldn't hear him, but still he yelled her name across the fields she was ploughing; his ma was a tough lady. She bought the house and the land when he was a babe. He had never met his father. "Died" was all his ma would say. Watching her, he felt so proud to be her boy. He was a man grown, with a job as a stone mason. John had built quite a reputation and was waiting for the day that one of the nobles commissioned him to build a folly. His real dream was to visit his birthplace. Sophie told him it was a gloomy place with an evil king. But he had found her drawings of wee cottages and streams with coloured fish and a castle that was the kind of building he could only dream of working on.

It had been a long day fixing the drystone wall of the garden. At least now the cattle couldn't stick their heads in the kitchen window and eat the pears. John knew there was more out there than this farm and the village. He wanted adventure. His ma had other ideas. She wanted him to wed one of the local girls and have babies. Build a nice house and live happily ever after.

Yuck!

John was aware he was handsome, with his dark hair that sat in waves to his shirt collar. He was well-built from all the masonry work, and every girl within a hundred miles dreamt of his green eyes. All he wanted was to experience more than the daily toil of work and admirers and really experience life.

~

KORF WAS FED UP; his brothers were all older, bigger, and meaner than him. Not that he was a wimp, far from it, but it got awfully tiresome being called Goldilocks and Kelly every chance they got. Lumbering to his feet, he decided to take a risk and go for a walk. This wasn't allowed during sunlight. Giants were slain on sight if the army was big enough.

Stupid people, always wanting to kill what is different from themselves.

His family was visiting the lowlands to gather straw and corn for later in the year. The myth that giants ate babies meant that the humans never thought of giants when their grain stores were a bit lower.

"Where you going, Kelly? Off to brush your hair?!"

Hank yelled from his seat near the cave mouth. Rolling his eyes, Korf just kept walking.

John heard the shout carried on the breeze. He was too far away to make out the words, but he was sure it was coming from Cain Rock. He wondered what he would do if he came across some smugglers.

Will I be able to subdue them? Take them to the square for justice? Shaking his head, he carried on along the road.

"Stupid lumbering idiot brothers, I wish they would go boil their heads," Korf grumbled as he stomped along the country lane, not caring who saw him.

Let them see the big scary Goldilocks. Pfft! Idiots the lot of them.

It was then that John appeared on the road before Korf. He had been daydreaming about his riches and fame for building a new keep for old King David. When he looked up and saw the biggest man he had ever seen—no . . . not a man . . . a GIANT; he was prepared to fight to the death. *There's no way I'm going to die from being struck down while running away.*

He charged forward.

Wonderful, an idiot human come to slay the big bad giant.

Korf watched as the man ran at him.

Moron.

Korf sat down in the middle of the lane and waited. John faltered; was he seriously sitting down? He certainly didn't look aggressive; in fact, he looked a tad bored and pissed off. Stowing his pickaxe at his hip, John approached at a more measured pace.

"What do you want? Want to make a name for yourself killing a giant?"

John was still a good ten feet away when he answered, "Not especially, no. I just don't fancy being killed by one while running for my life. It would shame my mother."

Korf chuckled. "Well, I guess we are in quite a pickle then. What is your name?"

"John. I am a stone mason. And you are?"

"Korf. I am the youngest son and no use to anyone."

It hit him like lightening: If he could get this giant to work with him behind the scenes, hewing stone from the cliffs and caves, he could build in half the time and maybe, just maybe, earn enough to see the land of his birth. He put the idea to Korf.

"So, we have an accord?" John held out his hand.

Korf just looked at him.

"You are meant to shake my hand, as a way of sealing the agreement."

Taking John around the middle Korf shook him up and down, then placed him back on shaking legs.

"Not quite what I meant!" John sat on the grassy verge and put his head between his knees.

Their arrangement worked better than they could ever have imagined. John rose in fame, and Korf was able to make his own wages. Life was good. Then the letter from The Royal House of David arrived that changed everything.

. . .

THE KING HAS GRANTED JOHN, MASTER STONE MASON, AN AUDIENCE AT HIS HUNTING LODGE ON THE SOUTH BANK OF THE OOGE RIVER. THE MEETING SHALL TAKE PLACE FOUR DAYS FROM THE DAY YOU RECEIVE THIS MISSIVE. DO NOT DISAPPOINT YOUR KING.

THAT NIGHT, John took the letter and read it to Korf. He explained that on this trip he would have to go alone. But as soon as he secured a commission, he would ride back for him. The king had left him a fine horse to use for the journey, so it would take no time at all. Korf just nodded and went back to hewing stone for their stores. He was content that John would not abandon him. They were friends, after all.

As soon as King David set eyes on the mason, he knew Hector (now long since dead) had lied to him. He had a good mind to dig the bastard up and throw his bones in the river, like he should have the boy all those years ago. Even aged, David was still as mean and power- hungry as ever. Though the fates seemed to favour him, why else would they allow him to cross paths with the boy again?

"I would very much like you to build me a new tower for my lady wife. She is wishing for a space to house her embroidery. She has quite outgrown the bower," King David said in an almost bored tone. Inside, though, he was seething with rage. He wanted to choke the man before him. However, looking at his frame it was but a dream.

John was beside himself with happiness and agreed to the commission at once.

"But I will need you to collect a few things for me before you start, mere trinkets if you will. I feel they would appease the queen while the noise and dust of the build is underway."

"Of course, Sire, name it, and I shall endeavour to fulfil the tasks," John replied, bowing low. The king smiled callously at the top of his opponent's head, for that is how he saw him.

"Good, good. Now, I need you to find a golden fruit that only grows in the mountains to the north, a jar filled with the water from the Well of Eternal Youth, and enough gold to make three strands of continuous chain, what we call the giants' style hair. Do all of that and not only will I have work start immediately, I will offer you my daughter's hand in marriage." David knew these were impossible tasks. It didn't matter. The fool would die trying.

TWO MONTHS LATER...

JOHN WAS ANNOYED. There was no such thing as the Well of Eternal Youth. There was no tree that bore golden fruit to the north. And he couldn't find gold anywhere that wasn't under the same king's protection. Knowing he had been duped, he was determined to find out why. Returning home, he went directly to his mother's house.

"Where have you been? That giant friend of yours is living in the barn now. Looters have taken up in his cave. It has been months, John!"

Her heart was filled with relief that he was alive, but she was so very angry at him. Disappearing and swearing that giant to tell no one where he had gone. How could he?

If nothing else, Korf was loyal.

"I met the king. He wanted to commission me to build

a tower for the queen, only he sent me on a wild goose chase that nearly got me killed on many occasions!"

This was not the greeting he had hoped for, but knew it was the one he deserved. Sophie felt the colour leave her cheeks. Once again, she was a fisher wife—well, maiden—down on the banks of the Ooge. She would never forget that day or the words the knight had spoken to her with such earnest. She had not taken them far enough. The tale of the babe's birth had reached her years later and with some digging she discovered a truth she never could have guessed.

"Sit, John, I need to explain things to you."

"KORF, I am in need of three of your hairs and do you happen to know where we might find some gold? Enough to cover an apple or pear?" John asked.

He had a plan and it was going to work. Korf nodded and allowed Sophie to cut three of his thick golden hairs from his head. She wound them like twine and put them into a leather bag. The next few hours were spent feeding stream water through pink clay to give it a slight colour and then adding one crusted quartz stone to make it shimmer. Korf found a nugget of gold and proved himself to be a pretty good goldsmith. The pear looked perfect.

John returned to the king within a week. He walked up to the throne and presented the items. King David was shocked and angry.

"Liar!" he screamed, "Fakes and lies! Guards!" "Before you do that, your majesty, I would like it to be known that my late father would not have approved of you treating your nephew in such a manner," John said calmly.

The news that he was indeed the son to the late and

would-be King William, had David not had him poisoned just days before his coronation, was a shock but also an opportunity. He had gotten messages to his mother who had been secreted away to a cottage with her handmaiden, Martha. It was when he had met her before coming here, and he had asked her to accompany him, that the plan was put in place.

"Lies!" King David was turning puce and tell-tale beads of sweat had collected at his temples.

John smiled. He had him.

"May I present my lady mother, Helen, wife to your rightful and sadly departed King William, the usurper's older brother?"

Helen was just as David remembered her. Those green cat-eyes gleamed with a secret triumph long- overdue to be paid in full. Helen then told her tale. Some of the staff still remembered that night and spoke up. The king was put in irons and thrown in the dungeons to live out the rest of his days.

John never did marry the princess. She and her mother left under peaceful terms. But he had had the adventure and now he was king. Lesson learned: Sometimes happily ever after is not about getting the girl, it's about fulfilling your dreams . . .

UGLY, BROKEN THINGS

BASED ON THE SIX SWANS

Dear Diary,

It has been three years since my father remarried, three years since I saw my home, and three years since I uttered a sound. The scars on my lips are still sore and red. I must scratch at them in the night. I can't be too careful. I still have nightmares of the day my bothers held me down and stitched my soft mouth closed, save for a tiny hole to push soft fruit through and sip at broth. I promised them I would never speak; I swore to it. Yet here I am, alone and living in the forest. I wish I could go home . . .

Eliana pushed her diary aside and looked out the window of her treehouse. She could just make out the top of the church spire. It glinted in the sunlight, mocking her. Why was her father such a stupid, self-centred man? Why had he married that hateful woman? Rising to her feet, she picked up her salve and applied it gingerly to her swollen lips. Her beauty was lost to her now. She would never marry; her brothers had seen to that.

She could hear her flock calling to her from the lake; the swans had been her constant companions since her family abandoned her. In that time, they had given birth to six beautiful cygnets. All were as white as snow, apart from wee Gerald; his grey baby plumage still clung to him in places. Eliana watched his siblings pull and pluck at him. She knew how poor Gerald felt. It was hard being the odd one out.

DEAR DIARY,

The king is the most loathsome man in the kingdom! After three years of marriage and the worst sex imaginable, it is no wonder I have never given him a son. My body is refusing to be infected with his seed. His six sons from his dead wife still loiter in corridors and beg for more gold, more attention, and better homes. They are never satisfied. It is my own fault, of course. I should not have made it known to them that I am an enchantress. I made them the men they are today. The price they paid was small and thanks to a little enchantment, not one of them remembers what they gave up to have their hearts' desires.

The Queen smiled as she closed her diary, and hid it once again behind the picture of the swans bathed in moonlight. The king would soon die if she had her way and the kingdom would pass to her. She would make sure of it.

DEAR DIARY,

Today I met a man. He tells me he is a king; he is handsome, but I do not want a king or a prince, I want to be able to sing again and smile. I threw the socks I had been darning at him until he left. Now I have to wash them all. The swans are restless again. I do hope they aren't thinking of leaving. My brothers were also in the forest today, hunting deer. Only one, the youngest and dearest to me came to my tree and threw me some chocolate. Simon is a good boy. Just sixteen, he is a man grown I suppose, but with his deformed arm he is for the church; there is no choice for him. I hate my father for that. Simon has as much right to marry and have children as the others. If I ever get free of this curse, I will help him. He reminds me of Gerald. Broken, ugly things often have the biggest hearts.

SIMON MISSED HIS SISTER; he had watched the day his other brothers had used the enchanted needle to sew her pretty mouth shut. He saw the moment the curse took hold. His brothers just walked away. To this day, they do not remember Eliana or what they did to her. He did, but he never let on. His stepmother was not to be angered, and he was mostly overlooked. Being a cripple had some advantages. Simon had a plan, and one day he would execute it.

The weeks turned into years, and the king died just as the enchantress predicted. All the sons renounced the throne, and so Magda became queen of the land. Eliana remained in her treehouse with her swans on the lake. Everyone just accepted the hand life had dealt them. Everyone except Simon. Now a full eighteen years old, he had left the church and travelled to a far-off kingdom. It was time to put his plan into action.

DEAR DAIRY,

Today the swans returned. I was so worried. They had been gone a full month and I feared I was to be truly alone. I have been collecting their feathers over the years. They are so beautiful and pearly white. I shall make myself a dress out of them. For my brothers, all except darling Simon, I shall make crowns from the grey feathers I kept from the cygnets. Ugly, dull headdresses for the ugliest and dullest men in the kingdom. I shall keep Gerald's beautiful silver feathers for

Simon; he has always been the silver lining to this prison. And like Gerald, he shines with a beauty that can only come from the heart.

It was a month later that Simon returned to Eliana's treehouse. He was sad to see his beautiful sister looking so beaten; she was losing hope. It was just as well that he had come bearing good news. The prince of the kingdom to which he had travelled had heard of the maiden living in a far-off forest. Simon told him that he knew of the maiden he spoke of and would take him to her, if in return, he would grant him a favour. The prince told Simon to name it, and it would be his. The deal was struck, and the two men took the fastest horses and headed for Eliana's forest.

DEAR DIARY,

Today is my wedding day. I know, it is hard for me to believe too. I have Simon to thank for this. He came to me, bringing a prince with him. At first, I wanted to turn them away. I did not want a prince. I did not need or want to marry. What could I offer a husband? I protested by throwing everything I owned at the poor man until I was left in nothing except my shift and my white feather gown, which I clutched to my chest.

He told me he knew of my tale and wanted to marry me. I looked into his eyes and knew him to be an honest man. But how could I leave my swans? Simon had thought of everything and said that there was a lake they could have just for themselves at the castle. So far, they have not followed me here, but I hold onto the hope that they will.

Eliana and PrinceAdam were married at sunset. She wore her swan feather gown and looked beautiful. Although she could not speak, Simon acted as her voice and made it known that when she regained her ability to speak, she would fill the kingdom with laugher and song. As the bride and groom drew close for an embrace, the guests cheered. Eliana's flock appeared, gliding low to the water's surface. It was the perfect end to the perfect day.

If only that were the end of the tale . . .

DEAR DIARY,

That whore Eliana is still alive! Worse, she has somehow managed to marry my distant cousin! Thank- fully his lady mother, my aunt, is still alive. I will end this marriage and kill the last spark of hope that whore has in her.

DEAR DIARY,

She's pregnant! Clearly my cousin was demented enough to want to put his cock into an ugly mute. I have conversed with my aunt. She has assured me I am not to worry, that she has a plan for Eliana and her tainted offspring. News has reached me that Simon is with her. He has been employed by Adam as a squire. Well it seems Adam has a liking for unwanted, broken things. His mother shall put paid to that.

Princess Eliana and Prince Adam, welcomed their first child, a boy, on the first day of Advent. He was perfect in every way. Queen Justine kept her distance from the child, claiming she was feeling frail and did not want to pass on the sickness to her darling grandson.

DEAR MAGDA,

. . .

THE CHILD HAS BEEN SECRETED AWAY BACK TO THAT DREADED FOREST AND TURNED INTO A SWAN. I WILL NOT KILL AN INNOCENT, AND ONLY MY DEATH WILL BREAK THE ENCHANTMENT. EVERY CHILD ELIANA BEARS WILL VANISH WITHIN THE FIRST MONTH OF LIFE. SHE WILL WAKE TO BLOOD SMEARED ON HER HANDS AND FACE. THE CRIB WILL BE BLOODIED AS WELL. IF MY SON DOES NOT THROW HER TO THE HANGMAN FOR THAT, I WILL BE AMAZED. IF NOTHING ELSE, ELIANA, THE WHORE, WILL GO INSANE. DO NOT WORRY MY NIECE, EVERYTHING IS IN HAND.

Justine

After the fourth child was taken, Eliana was ready to die. Adam was in deep mourning, and the kingdom whispered of the mad princess who killed and drank the blood of her babies. The queen called for her death, and so Eliana, mute and broken, waited to be killed.

DEAR DIARY,

Today I will be put to death and I welcome it. Simon has gone to fetch our brothers and stepmother. It appears that Queen Justine wishes this to be a family event. How touching. My darling Adam is a broken man. I promised him song and laughter. All I have brought him is pain. I do not deserve his love, as I did not deserve my children. I am an ugly, broken thing; it is right that I should be thrown away and forgotten.

The Hangman waited for his signal. Prince Adam turned away. He did not believe his wife had killed their children, but he could not explain away the evidence. Queen Justine and Queen Magda stood side by side. Stone-faced were they, but the glint in their cruel eyes told a story of triumph. The crowd parted and Simon appeared. In his hands were the five grey crowns Eliana had made for her bothers. He climbed the ladder to the platform where his sister stood and produced a needle. Confused, Eliana looked at her brother with dead eyes. Smiling, Simon touched the needle to his sister's lips. The stitches disappeared. With her voice restored to her, Eliana yelled at the top of her lungs for her brothers to be brought forward. The five men were presented to her. Even with the rough noose around her neck, Eliana had never looked more beautiful or fierce. She asked Simon to place the crowns on their heads. It was her last gift to her kin.

Queen Magda went pale. The whore could speak, and she knew full-well what she had done to her all those years ago. Beginning to back out of the royal seating area, she found herself trapped by a line of palace guards— guards loyal to Prince Adam.

Eliana told her tale, and Queen Magda was taken to the dungeon, where her mouth was stitched closed with the same needle she had had her stepsons use on Eliana. As soon as the last stitch was in place, the enchantment over her brothers was lifted.

Queen Justine was incensed. How dare they do that to her niece—this girl was a nobody! She would not have the people's love; she would not have one more day alive to spread her vile poison. Lifting her arms, she began to curse the princess. Simon, who had donned his silver crown, removed the dagger he carried in his boot and struck the bitch between the eyes. What happened next was too extraordinary for words.

DEAR DIARY,

Today I sit with my babies. They are perfect and whole. Adam and I are so glad to have them back. I knew they were not dead. Queen Justine's magical hold on them was lost the moment she died. However, it seems that something even stranger took place that day. The moment she died my five brothers vanished. Simon dropped to the ground and was taken to the healer. I have been told his deformed arm is now whole and as strong as his right.

I cannot say I am sad that these things have happened. Maybe sometimes broken things are there to teach others how to appreciate what they have. I wish no ill will to my brothers wherever they are. Now, Adam and I will concentrate on our children and live happily together as a family should.

QUEEN MAGDA DIED many years later, mute and alone. The enchanted needle was hidden away so as never to be used against another ever again. And Queen Eliana was much beloved by her people. Simon married a gentle woman and was often a visitor at the castle. His plan came together perfectly. He knew all that throwing practice would come in useful one day. As for the five brothers, there are five new swans on the forest lake by Eliana's treehouse. They are full grown, but their feathers are an ugly, dull grey.

DULL FEATHERS

BASED ON THE UGLY DUCKLING

Beauty is in the eye of the beholder, yes? Well if that is true, why are so many judged for their appearance? It is an interesting topic, beauty, who has it, who doesn't, what it looks like, and what it sounds like. Who gets to say what it beautiful and what is not? It was decided on the day of my birth that I was ugly. It sounds terrible doesn't it, hearing that a child brand new to the world was declared ugly. Not by the mother, my mother no, she never got to see me. I was declared hideous by the very people who brought me into the world. I know others might think that this cannot be true; no doctor or midwife would ever deem a child that repulsive as to categorise it as ugly only moments after birth. Well, it is true, and it happened to me; the worst part is they took it one terrifying step further. After the sound of my cry broke the silence of the birthing room and my mother's exhausted plea to hold her child, the doctors told her no, and the midwife took her hand as two new members of staff entered the room. Ones she had never seen before.

"Your baby is very sick; we must take him to a special

care baby unit right away." Of course my mother let them, it was in my best interest, wasn't it? As far as she knew, I was dying. If only that had been the case.

I never saw my mother; I don't even know what her name is. I was never taken back to her. I found out years later when I began my search that they had told her I had died shortly after being admitted to the special care baby unit. For unknown reasons, maybe grief, she never came to view my little body. I am sure, knowing what I know now, that there would have been a tiny perfect baby for her to weep over. The lost child of another mother in the unit I never went to. This is the problem. Sometimes those in power can have such sway over us that we believe them without question.

As I grew, I didn't notice my differences; I was surrounded by others who I learned later, were like me, extraordinary. You see, it wasn't something that entered our heads, to question it. To consider ourselves freakish or ugly was the last thing we would have thought. Each and every one of us in the dormitory was unique.

I was around six years old when I was taken for my first investigation, the nurse who looked after us all, Wendy, explained to me that I was going to help the doctors and nurses understand how special I was. I smiled and was willing to help in any way I could; if Wendy was telling me I was special then it must be true. She was very kind to us all, always bringing us treats and new books to read.

I will never forget that day though, the day that Wendy lied to me for the first time. That's unfair, she had omitted to tell me the whole truth. The doctors and nurses really did want to look at me, to study me and learn all about it. Unfortunately, it was the way in which they wanted to investigate my specialness that was the problem.

The room I was taken to was very clean; the smell of

bleach burned my nose. My name is Elijah; I am a boy, and I am tall for my age, or so I'm told. My specialness is that I have an extremely good sense of smell. My eyesight is also hypersensitive to the point where I have to wear special glasses with dark blue lenses all the time. I have never seen my eyes; when I have tried to look in the mirror the light reflecting off the shiny surface causes me extreme pain, though, I know from asking my friend Sophie in the dormitory that my eyes are a vivid red. I also have incredibly thin skin. This means that it is possible to see almost all of my internal organs without the need for medical equipment. It does freak out the other kids at first, usually the younger ones, but they soon see the cool side to it. Due to my translucent skin, I have to be very careful about what touches it. I can only tolerate thin clothing, as even cotton causes friction burns and bleeding. I don't really have hair, just a few tuffs around my ears. When Wendy took me into this very white, very clean, and very large room, I began to wonder what exactly was going to happen to me that day.

"Elijah, why don't you come sit in this chair for me," she said, all the while smiling at me.

I nodded and almost skipped to the large plastic covered chair in the centre of the room. I took a moment to take in my surroundings fully and noticed that about two thirds of the way up the white titled walls were huge windows. I'd hoped to see the sky; I wasn't allowed outside much due to my skin condition. It burned incredibly easily. However, instead of seeing the endless blue of fluffy clouds, I saw faces. Not faces like mine or my friends, but faces like Dr. Smithson's and Wendy's, these types of faces I learned later on are what society consider acceptable and beautiful. Most importantly, I learned that these faces were "normal". At the time, I was just extremely pleased to see so many people, people who wanted to see me, and to admire my specialness.

Dr. Smithson was over by a huge monitor. I could hear him tapping keys on a keyboard that I couldn't see. I really liked Dr. Smithson; he was kind, with a big smile and a funny little beard that reminded me of the tuft of hair on the back of my head. I was so busy taking in the sounds and the faces that looked down on me from above that I didn't notice the other person in the room. This person was another nurse, I think. I never really saw them; they seemed to almost sneak up on me from behind. I had only had time to notice her bright blue eyes before I felt a very sharp pain in my right arm. A few seconds later, the room went fuzzy and the people in the viewing gallery seemed to almost disappear. I wanted to call them back, to tell them that I was sorry if I had done something wrong and I would promise to be good. Unfortunately, I didn't seem to be able to speak and then there was nothing at all.

This happened over and over again to me and to my friends in the dormitory. Some never came back, and when we lost one friend, a new child would appear within a few months, usually to take their place. There were never more than thirteen of us in the dormitory at one time, even though there were fourteen beds. When I asked Wendy about this she told us that it was because if one of us got very poorly she would need somewhere to sleep.

My friends and I grew close as the years went by, growing and learning together in our sunny ward that was surrounded by green fields and tall trees. If it weren't for the constant investigations and the memory loss that followed, it would have been the perfect place to live.

I wish I could remember the things that were done to me during my visits to the observatory/operating theatre; my only reminders of my time spent in there were sore patches on my skin and on two occasions, temporary blindness that lasted a month.

Then one day completely out of the blue when I was around twelve—no, no, I was much older—I forget how long I spent there, you see the days all seemed to blend into one. Anyway, it was coming close to Christmas, I remember that much. My friend Sophie hadn't come back from her latest visit with Dr. Smithson, and I was upset. It seemed lately that too many of my friends were not coming back from these studies, as the doctor called them. I looked around the room, and only seven beds, including my own, were now occupied. It was with sadness that I realised we had lost six of our friends in the last four weeks.

That day proved to be different. That day, new people came to see us in the ward, as that's what we learned it was, not a nice dormitory, a hospital ward. These people were policemen, new doctors, and others who wore suits. They all had kind faces. I later learned that the ones in suits were social workers and government officials. They took us all away that day, treated the wounds on those of us that had them, fed us food we had never tasted before, and gave us clean clothes and toys for the younger ones. Everything seemed fine; we were happy, warm, and felt safe, especially once we were told that we would never have to experience any more of Dr. Smithson's special studies ever again.

Things almost went to hell when they tried to separate us. They didn't understand that since we had always been together and now that we understood that strangers and "normal" people could hurt us and steal our friends away, we were desperate to stay together. We were family. So when the social workers came to tell us we were to be fostered with families that we could call our very own, an uproar broke out. We told them we didn't want a new home or family. We had a family; we were all each other had.

The problem, as it usually is in the eyes of those in charge, was the law of the land. We were not heard; we were children, and they knew what was best for us. So, we were each given time to say goodbye and then each of us was taken by gentle hands to our new families to start the business of living a "normal" life.

Thankfully, we were able to keep in touch. Our new families understood our bond and didn't want to steal that away, so once a month we all met up and exchanged stories and experiences. The most special moments were birthdays because each year we got to celebrate seven rather than wondering who would be missing that year.

My start in life and those of my friends was not conventional; it wasn't even close to "normal". However, it did teach us a lot. The idea of beauty is seen at face value; this is an extremely narrow way of viewing what is one of the most complex and amazing attributes the human race possesses.

Beauty is not just what you look like—it is who you are. It is your actions, the challenges you undertake, and the struggles you overcome. The words you speak into your life, not the judgment of those around you, determine a great deal of your beauty as a human. Words are the most powerful force on the planet.

I look different; I am unique and yet, so is everyone else. So, if we all share this common denominator of uniqueness, then surely we are all the same? That is a positive way to view the world, isn't it? We are all human, whether we are tall or short, reed thin or strapping and broad. We all have a heartbeat. We all have feelings and a great capacity for love as well as hate.

My favourite book that nurse Wendy used to read to us

in the ward every Friday was a book about a swan who landed in the wrong nest before he had even hatched and was then shunned by his new family because he was different. My favourite part was always the shock of the duck family when the ugly duckling was revealed to be a swan. How beautiful they found him after his dull feathers had been replaced by snowy white ones.

That story taught me that you should never shun anyone because of their differences. Like the ugly duckling, sometimes they just need a chance to grow. That people need to look past the superficial and truly see what's there.

My name is Elijah. I am a hypersensitive albino with alopecia. However, those differences do not make me any less beautiful. They do not define me as the man I have grown to be. They are things I have, not who I am. Just like the duckling in my favourite childhood book, my outward appearance may not be to the world's standard of beauty, but I will surprise them, the naysayers. I am much more than meets the eye.

BAKLAVA AND WISHES

BASED ON THE LITTLE MATCH GIRL

Molly was cold, and her skirt was wet from the snow and ice. She had been looking for her kitten when she became lost, and now, as the lamp lighters took to the slushy streets, she really became scared. Having only been in England a few weeks, she did not know how to ask for help. Oma had told her not to leave the front yard. But her kitten, Fleur, had darted out the gate at the sound of a dog barking. Molly feared her kitten would be trampled by a horse or flattened by a cartwheel. She had called to her Oma before she ran after Fleur.

It had been light then; the crisp air of the last day of December stung her cheeks, making them rosy. She looked all over. Her hose and skirt soon became soaked, and her feet were already numb from the icy water that found its way in through tiny holes in the seams of her boots. Now, the sky was an indigo blue and the air was much colder than before. Wrapping her arms around herself, she hurried from each new pool of light cast by the hissing gas lamps. Oma would be so worried, and Molly was hungry. Fleur was still nowhere to be found.

I wish I were at home with Oma. She would have made baklava and hot milk. Molly watched other children with their parents and wished hers were here and not in Amsterdam with her brother Daan. She had only her Oma and now she had lost her too, in this new land where she could not ask for help. She had tried, but it was no use.

"Ik ben verdwaald!" *I am lost, help me!*

She had pleaded to the lady wearing a moss green coat. "I am sorry, dear. I don't understand," was the reply she received. If only she knew English.

The night grew colder still; the streets growing empty, as families took to their dinner tables to enjoy the last meal of the year. Her tummy rumbled; she was so tired and cold, and her small hands were turning blue. Sitting in a doorway, she cupped her hands and blew hot breath into them. It was then that she heard the scuffle and breaking glass. Scared of what danger might lurk in the shadows, Molly ran.

Oma Tess was worried. Molly had been gone a long time. She had searched the streets and been to the police, but with it being a holiday, there were few who wanted to listen to an old Dutch grandma. She was grateful that one of the people she had asked understood her. It was rare in this country to find a fellow Dutch speaker.

Where is my Molly? She is all I have in this world.

It was a painful secret that Tess kept hidden from the child. Her parents and bother would never come across the sea to England. There had been an outbreak of pox, and to save their daughter they had sent her to England with her only living grandparent. Daan had shown the early signs, and they knew that he would not survive it. He had always been a sickly boy. A telegram had arrived the week after they had arrived in London.

TESS DE VRIES.
YOUR GRANDSON DAAN DE VRIES IS DEAD. HIS PARENTS EMMA AND JACOB HAVE BOTH TAKEN ILL WITH THE POX.

THE LITTLE SLIP of paper broke her heart. Even written in English, she could understand that her beautiful grandson would never bring her paintings of tulips again or ask to make baklava. Molly loved her brother more than anything and for that reason she would not tell her— not yet. Now she must find her granddaughter before something terrible happened to her. So out into the bitter December night, Oma Tess went to find the little girl she loved most.

MOLLY WANTED TO CRY, but she knew the tears would just cause her cheeks to sting even more. She held them in.

I *want my Oma; I want my Fleur and my bed with the pink blanket Mama made for me.*

The wind whipped her russet curls into a wet, matted mess. Lamp light spilled onto the street through gaps in the curtains of the homes she passed. When she was able, she peeked in. She saw tables laden with food and families sitting around the fire. How she missed her family. Her brother would be playing with his big red truck on the kitchen floor, and Mama would be making spiced apples for pudding. Onward she walked; the snow falling harder, and the streets all blurring into one unknown tunnel of white. "Oma! Oma!" Molly called out into the night. The wind stole her words and pressed her sodden skirt to her cold legs. It was then that she saw a little ginger body sitting just a few feet ahead of her.

"Fleur! Oh, where have you been?"

She ran and scooped up her kitten. Reaching up to her hair, Molly untied the two yellow ribbons holding her curls off her face and tied one around Fleur's slender neck. "Clever kitten, take us home to Oma Tess." She put the warm kitten back on the ground and followed her through the snow.

The small house appeared amid the snow, and the candle was burning bright in the window. Molly and Fleur ran up the short path and pushed the latch on the door. It was locked.

"Oma must have gone out looking for me," she gasped.

Fleur was yowling for food. Looking at the house, Molly saw the kitchen window was open a crack. Finding an old plant pot, she stood on its slippery base and pulled the window open enough to push Fleur through.

"I will be back soon, little cat, be a good girl now," she whispered, before pushing the window closed. Now I must find my Oma. She once again headed out into the unknown streets.

The church bells began to toll the half hour, and Oma Tess was tired. She had walked to the river and up to the park. Molly was not there. It was as she passed by the butcher's shop, that she saw something yellow poking out of the snow. *Molly used hair ribbons of this colour today. Maybe she has found her way home; it is not far from here.* Quickening her pace, Tess hurried back to her home and prayed she would find her granddaughter there.

Molly and Oma met at the gate of the house; Molly had not gone more than two streets when she realised that the right thing to do was to wait by the house for Oma to return. They held each other close as they made their way into the small house. Fleur was waiting for them and yowling for her supper.

"Go wash your hands and face, sweet one. I shall warm you a nightgown by the fire." Oma pushed the shivering Molly toward the stairs.

"But Oma, you are so cold, I can see your lips are blue. Please go and get changed first, I can light the fire," the little girl said.

"Do not fret, sweet girl, I am strong. You go on and I shall go next once I have fed the cat," Oma Tess assured the child.

Dry and warming by the fire, the family of two shared a mug of hot milk and baklava, just as Molly had known they would. The bells began to toll. The new year had arrived. "Gelukkig nieuwjaar, Oma!"

But Oma Tess was asleep. The sweet treat was still in her hand. "Oma. It is the new year, our first in this country. Tomorrow we must go to the river and drink the water, and we have to burn our wishes for the coming year . . . Oma?"

Molly was scared. She had seen death before and knew that Oma was dead. *No, maybe she is just cold,* she thought, knowing it was not true. She ran to her room and pulled the pink blanket from her small bed and covered Oma Tess with it. The cheery colour only made the blue of her grandmother's skin all the more obvious.

"I shall just burn our wishes on the candle then, Oma, and come rest with you. In the morning, I shall make you breakfast, and the day will be sunny and full of joy," Molly whispered through her silent tears. Taking the small slips of paper from the special plate that was always used for wishes, little Molly from Amsterdam burned the wishes of two refugees on the first day of the new year.

Laying down beside her Oma, Molly kissed her cold cheek. "Sweet dreams, Oma."

The New Years Day tragedy was the talk of the street. Tess and Molly De Vries had died in the night. The police said their chimney became packed with soot and they died from the smoke that filled the small house. Others claimed they had brought a foreign disease with them and God had punished them by killing them both.

"Burn the house!"

"Cleanse this street of the plague."

There was never a burning of the house. A new family moved in, a young girl and her parents. They even looked after Fleur as she had managed to find a way out and had survived, but always returned to the house.

The new family was also Dutch, and their daughter was to sell the bundles of matches that her parents made. It was a thriving business, and the child was soon known well in the community. She knew what had happened to the last family, and every night before bed, the little match girl would burn a wish for the Oma and her grandchild. The wish was always the same:

Let them be together and let there always be a warm
fire and a candle to light their way.

FOREVER YOUNG

BASED ON SNOW WHITE AND ROSE RED

Lillie and Rose were fighting again. Their mother was at her wit's end. *Why can't they get along like they did as children?*

The screaming reached its peak. There was the sound of breaking glass and then the door slammed shut. Karen flinched at the sounds and braced for whichever angry teen was about to burst into the parlour.

"Mother, she is the Devil's own I swear it by the Goddess."

"Rose, she is your sister. Being a twin is a special gift.

I don't understand why you fight so much."

"Because she is a slovenly, rude twit, and I am fed up with always being the 'kind' one. Just because she has that black hair and porcelain skin, I am forever cast aside. Do you know how many courters she has?"

Rose was lost to her anger. Her blonde hair flew, and her rosebud mouth turned down in a sullen pout. Even then she looked beautiful. Karen sighed and continued her sewing. If only their father were still alive. To be left alone with two twin girls on the brink of womanhood seemed deeply unfair to the widow.

"I am going for a walk," Rose continued. "I need to be away from her before I do something she will regret."

I love my children. I love my children, Karen repeated to herself long after the front door slammed and the sound of Lillie playing the lute filtered down to her. She needed a way to get them to realise how important having a twin was. She began to form a plan for her two tempestuous teens.

Lillie was also angry. She was the kind of angry that she could taste. Rose was becoming an even bigger pain in the ass than usual. It's not like she knew anything; it's not like Henry had promised to marry her. It wasn't her fault that he liked her more. But Rose would never see it that way. Not that she would ever know the truth. When had they become enemies? She couldn't remember a particular event that had turned sister against sister. Maybe it was just what happened when you were sixteen and still sharing a room.

~

"HAPPY BIRTHDAY, GIRLS."

A small cake was placed between the two eighteen-year-olds. Today her plan was finally ready. The last two years had been a war zone in the house with each girl getting more and more out of control. But now they would learn. At least she hoped they would.

The two beautiful young women glared at each other; even on their birthday it was impossible to stay civil for long. Sensing another argument, Karen coaxed the girls out of the house. On the old tree stump were two bags, two cloaks, and two purses of silver.

"This is my gift to you two. Get out."

They watched shocked as their mother turned back to the house and shut the door, sliding the bolt into place. The twins just stood there dumbfounded. It hurt so much to see them out there alone, but this had to be done. She was fed up with living in a home full of conflict and being cook and cleaner for those two. They were old enough now. Time to grow up.

"Mother has lost her mind," Lillie gasped, staring at the tree stump and then back at her childhood home.

"This isn't at all funny. She can't mean it?" Rose laughed nervously. Mother was just not this much of a bitch, that was Lillie's department. Lillie and Rose felt suddenly very alone and not at all prepared for the world they had been thrust into. Wanting to save face, Rose picked up her share of the "gifts" and turned to her sister.

"Well, goodbye. Have a wonderful life."

THE YEARS WENT by and the twins never saw each other again. Their mother died in a flash flood and neither girl knew. Anger and pride had eaten away at them until their beauty was taken from them and their youth was all but a memory.

Lillie had married a baker and had seven children, all boys. She was happy enough, but the bitterness in her heart was too engrained for her to feel real joy. Rose had married a blacksmith. She had not been blessed with children. The couple had inherited a cottage when the smith's grandmother had died in a freak wolf attack.

That was until the day of the storm. A great thunderstorm ripped through the land. Trees caught fire and farmsteads burned to ashes. The smith and the baker were called to help with the rescue of a young family trapped in a farmhouse. They had never crossed paths, being from different villages. The strange thing was, they were identical. Once the fire was out and the family safe, John the baker and Philip the smith sat with a cup of ale and discovered everything about each other, including their wives. Deciding to play a trick on their wives, the men agreed to swap places to see if they could raise a smile from the once beautiful women. Little did they know, a mother's magic was finally taking hold.

Philip returned home with a gnome for Lillie's garden and toffee apples for the children. John returned home to Rose with a bear skin. Neither woman suspected the man she was with was not her husband. The seemingly barren Rose even fell pregnant, and the petulant Lillie discovered laughter again. Slowly, the women's beauty returned to them.

But it just so happens, that sometimes the enchantment can get bent out of shape, and the caster of this spell was long since dead. The men began to age at an astonishing rate, while the two sisters became younger and more beautiful. On the day of their thirtieth birthday, the men met up once again at the same spot. Both looked to be in their dotage.

"What has happened to us?" they asked, shocked to discover the affliction was upon them both. "Your wife has not aged a day; her beauty is beyond compare,"

John said.

"Your wife is also beautiful and full of laughter. She had a child, and the light that shines from her now is so radiant," Philip whispered as he stared at the man so changed like himself.

The men then realised that they had been living a lie for years. They needed to return to their original wives. The trouble was they had fallen in love with the ones they had more recently been with. Both still remembered the sour women they had ran from; they had been shrews. Agreeing to one more week before the switch, the men parted ways.

The women were once again unaware of the switch and carried on their lives as normal. But as the days went on, their beauty began to fade. They became bitter again, and their husbands returned to their virile selves.

Knowing something was amiss, Lillie and Rose followed the men a month later. Imagine their shock when they saw that they had married identical men—right down to the curve of their crooked smiles. It was also the first time they had seen each other in many years. They were both stunned at the aged wreck the other had become. Deciding to confront the men, the women came out of their hiding places. The closer they got to each other, the more their youth returned to them. Magic cast long ago was finally coming full circle.

"How is this possible?" they gasped, though the distance did not allow their voices to carry. Their matching expressions spoke a thousand words.

"Ladies, we can explain . . ." the men blustered as wrinkles and white hair began to appear once more. The sisters didn't care; they just wanted to keep getting younger. The youth and beauty that was being restored to them came with knowledge, a deep understanding that when they held onto hate and anger, they reflected it. When they loved and laughed, they reflected that also. The men began to age more rapidly as the women got closer and closer.

"Lillie, I have missed you." "Rose, I am so sorry."

The two women reached out tentative hands. When their fingers touched, a brilliant light shone from between them. John and Philip screamed in pain. The sisters turned to see their husbands lying dead on the ground, as old and wizened as grandfathers.

The two women returned to Lillie's home and together raised their eight children. Once the children were grown, the women went in search of more doppelgängers. They had researched the magic that had been cast upon them. Their new hatred was not for each other. No, now their bitterness was reserved strictly for men. Men had wronged them, and men must pay. So, they toured the lands searching for men to ensnare and share.

Their mother, on trying to bring her sweet girls back, had managed to create two vengeful witches. To this day they wander the earth never getting older, searching out doppelgängers to trap and punish.

Sometimes happy ever after is just a fairy tale. Sometimes it's deadly.

THE ARTIST

BASED ON THE GIANT WHO HAD NO HEART IN HIS BODY

Augustine had never been average. He was always tall for his age and unnervingly smart. The thing that really freaked out his parents, and later the many therapists he would see, was his obsession with wax.

Not *too* unhealthy you might think. Ordinarily you would be correct. But Augustine's obsession was more sinister than just "I love the feel of it" or the act of melting wax. Instead, he liked to encase things within it.

It started with a candle kit his auntie bought him for his eighth birthday. He accidentally dropped a paperclip into the wax mould. When the candle was complete, he gave it to his mother to light. As the wax melted away, the paper clip revealed itself, as if it were a treasure. After that, Augustine began to make his treasure candles every week. His parents bought him wax and new moulds. They were just pleased that he was happy.

It was as he grew that the treasures became a bit disturbing. First was a spider. He killed it and then carefully positioned its legs in the wax so that as it burned, the spider looked like it was praying. Next came mice. It was after *that* incident—the one with the mouse who starved to death because he couldn't get away—that his parents took him to see a shrink. They hoped it would fix everything and give him the help they thought he needed.

But Augustine was the model patient. He told Dr. Fields exactly what he wanted to hear so that he could quit the sessions. And that's precisely what happened. Only ten sessions in, Dr. Fields told the boy's parents there was nothing wrong with him and called it all a phase.

But it wasn't. When he reached seventeen, he got a job in the local craft shop and spent his wages on bigger moulds and more wax. The fascination was too engrained, and Augustine wanted to experiment. At almost seven feet tall and as broad as a doorway, Augustine was an intimidating sight. The coaches at school begged him to join the football team, basketball, and even wrestling. Every request was met with a solid "no". He had his wax and his experiments. They were all he needed.

At nineteen, when he had finally moved out of his parents' home, Augustine encased his first cat in wax. The result was not as he wanted. The smell was horrific, and the wax did not take well to the feline fur. There was only one way to rectify this, and further experiments were undertaken using cats from the neighbourhood. The locals were up in arms. Neighbourhood pets were going missing, and no one could work out why.

With the encasement of cats perfected, but still craving more, Augustine paid no attention to the locals and instead took time to study embalming. He was ready for something bigger. Much bigger.

His first murder was sloppy. It was of a child he had come across at the park. He had been looking for a short woman as the mould he had was only five feet tall. So, when the little girl came over to him, her eyes filled with tears asking if he knew where her mummy had gone, Augustine made a quick calculation and snatched her.

Like with the cats, the first attempt did not go as planned. Being a large man, he had considerable strength and accidentally crushed the child's skull. With her head misshapen and blood mixing with the wax, it was all a bit of a mess. But Augustine was stubborn. This did not put him off. Instead, he took his notes and decided that next time he would use a less bloody method of killing. Plus, in all his excitement to test his mould, he had not embalmed her. Another lesson learned. Next time would be different.

Over the next four years, Augustine perfected his chosen art. That was how he saw his practice, as an art form. The homeless were a great starting point. The missing kid had caused a bit of a circus, and he really didn't need that kind of attention. That was the past. Now he was ready to begin his greatest project yet.

He met the first woman at a bar. She was drunk and flirting with anyone who stood still long enough. The thought of being that desperate was just beyond him. Augustine had no sexual desires. Never had. This is what the police were getting so wrong. They believed the crimes where sexually motivated, like he was some kind of deviant. Augustine considered himself to be the creator of art: Taking something ugly and unwanted and making it beautiful.

The drunk woman was almost *too* easy. She got into a cab with him and went to his home, stripped herself naked and rested on his sofa. Augustine was repulsed. Thanks to the amount of alcohol she had poured down her throat, her death was quick.

Embalming takes an hour, so when he was done, Augustine went and had a cup of coffee and a cookie. It was the little things in life that pleased him. Cookies with just chocolate—no nuts. Other favourite things of his were rain on his roof while he laid in bed and of course, his projects. But cookies, they were the best of all.

"You will be the start of my exhibit," he said to the woman lying on his mortician's slab an hour later. Augustine was more than just a killer and an artist. He was a trained mortician. After the unfortunate accident with the kid, he decided the best way to become a master of his craft was to practice the preparation on consenting—sort of—adults.

The mould was ready. He double-checked everything to make sure he was correct on his calculations. Augustine was never wrong, but *arrogance was what would get him caught.* That was a fact he was sure of. So, he always checked just for good measure. The thick chain was already around the woman's ankles. Once attached to the winch, Augustine lowered his subject into the hot wax in the six-foot mould he had had made especially for this project. This mould was special. The inside was etched with patterns and text. Little quotes that would be thought-provoking, or so Augustine hoped. This was more than a candle. This was a statement.

The end result was more than he could have hoped for. She was breathtaking when she came out of the mould; the etchings making her more beautiful than she had ever been in life. Once she was stored safely, Augustine cleaned his workspace and went to bed. Tomorrow, he was going to acquire number two.

The next few weeks passed in a happy blur. The women were easier to obtain then he imagined. He never learned their names. They were his subjects. Art materials. Names did not matter, only the finished piece. With six girls, all stored, and the art gallery booked for his anonymous debut, there was no way he was going to attend. *That* would get him caught. Anyway, he wanted the art to make the impact, not him.

That night, he went out to find lucky number seven. The final piece for his seven deadly sins exhibition. He felt on top of the world. He was about to complete a never-before-seen art form. The crowds were going to love it. It's not like people were against dead things being used in art. What about that artist who had a cow chopped in half, suspended in formaldehyde, and put in the Tate Modern? People flocked to see that. This would be a hit. He just knew it.

He was going to search the crowds at the biggest night club in town—PULSE. The girls there were always plentiful, and the dark areas of the club made for the perfect place to observe and not get chatted up. He knew where all the fire exits were and how many were alarmed. This would be easy.

It was just after ten when he spotted "the one." She was around five feet six inches without her heels. She had red hair and green eyes. Not that it mattered, really, not to begin with. She had great curves and a beautiful face that was angular and sharp. *Almost feline,* he thought. Augustine watched her from the upper balcony. His idea to hide out was stopped when a bouncer by the name of Steve told him to "Buy a drink and mingle or get the hell out."

She appeared to be alone, but anxious. This was a complication, but not the end of the world. He would just have to change tactics and get her outside. Just as he was making his way down to her, she grabbed her phone from the table in front of her and headed for the door. Fate was on his side. Augustine moved swiftly through the crowded club and out into the sea air. She was heading toward the pier. *Perfect.* The sound of the high tide would drown out any struggle, and with holiday season over, well, he was not likely to be seen either. She was on the phone when he grabbed her. The caller wouldn't have heard anything other than the phone hitting the floor. Augustine was well-practiced in moving a captive, but making it look like they were together. Taking her home in his arms went completely unnoticed, which was just how he liked to do things.

Conner was freaked out. Flick had been on the phone with him, listening to him beg for forgiveness; he was having to stay late at work again and miss date night. She was totally chewing him out, and then, nothing. There was a clatter and the phone went dead.

Conner searched for Flick for two days before he got a lead. Someone had seen her at the club—a waitress called Winter. She was coming back from her break and recognised Conner and asked where his girlfriend was. It was then he learned of the creepy guy hanging out in dark corners. She remembered seeing Flick leave and creeper guy leaving right after.

This did not make Conner feel better. It was easier to believe that she had gone to one of the hotels for a couple of days to let him sweat. Or to that dragon of a mother of hers who lived in Christchurch Village. This was his worst nightmare. Someone had Flick, and he knew that this creepy guy, as Winter called him, was the prime suspect. Luck was on his side that day too. When Scarlet, another waitress, came in for afternoon prep, she told them about this big guy who was living in Mrs. Jerkins' house in the old town. He had "dead eyes," she said, and that was enough for Conner to be sure this guy was bad news.

. . .

Augustine was disappointed. The last mould he made for lucky number seven was faulty. It had taken him two days to fix it. That was two days too long with a live subject. She wouldn't stop staring at him. The blind- fold made no difference. No, he couldn't see her eyes, but he still felt them on him. Judging him. This is why he acquired, killed, and transformed in a short amount of time.

The sound of the front door made him jump. Who was knocking on his door? He knew no one, and he entered though the rear of the house. The front was a mess. To give out the "go away, you are not welcome" vibe. So far it had worked. Some moron clearly thought that it was a challenge, or was just super unobservant. Either way it was a distraction he didn't appreciate.

Conner knocked hard on the filthy door and ran back down the path and toward the rear of the house. That was where Scarlet had said she saw him. Looking at the front, Conner was guessing the back was the way he usually used. He checked that his gun was still wedged in his belt. He might be a cop, but this was not an official call, and he should not have his gun on him at all. This would get him fired. But if it meant getting Flick out of this alive, he really didn't care.

Augustine opened the door; there was no one there. He was expecting the local teenage populous trying to sell the street something useless, stolen car radios or knocked off trainers. Annoyed to have been disturbed, he slammed the door, locked it, and headed back to his basement workroom. The sight he found when he got there was shocking. There was a man in his home. In his work area. *Touching* his materials. The girl was untied and biting her lip to stop her screams, or so he guessed. The second she spotted him, the sound that ripped from her was deafening. The man turned and pointed a gun at Augustine.

There was no exchange, no snappy comebacks to well-thought-out one-liners. Just the sound of the gun echoing off of the tiled walls. It took a second for the pain to register. Augustine had taken two bullets to the chest. His heart lurched. The shooter was turning to leave. In an instant, the girl took the gun and shot him again. This one pierced his heart. The last thing he saw before death took his soul to hell, were the storage chests containing his most prized possessions. His wax works.

Conner turned to Flick.

"Why did you kill him? I was going to call it in."

Flick would tell Conner all about the wax and the plans that monster had had for her, but for now she simply answered.

"Because he deserved it."

LUCIFER'S WIFE

BASED ON THE GIRL WITHOUT HANDS

I want to tell you my story, the story of why I mutilated myself. You see, I believed the devil was after me and wanted me for his bride. So, I tried to be as good as any person can be on this corrupted planet to keep him at bay. The lengths I had to go to may shock you. But would you not fight for your freedom even if it meant losing a part of yourself?

My name is Amelia. I am an only child. My mother left when I was a tiny babe in arms and my father was the worst kind of man—fuelled by lust, money, and alcohol. My childhood was hard. The beatings came often, and I was always hungry and cold.

When I was around six, a man came to me in my dreams. He had long black hair studded with diamonds and a face so handsome that even then I was captivated by him. He told me his name was Lucifer and that one day he would come for me. I believed him.

All through my teenage years I dreamed of him. I performed sex acts with other men while I pictured his face. My father, a devout Christian, was concerned that I was dressing provocatively and had me attend mass every week in the hope of cleansing me of the evil he saw within me. I never told him that Lucifer came to me almost every day. That he loved me above all others and wanted to make me his queen. I know, looking back I was off my head, but at the time it was real, and I wanted him.

It was not long after that my father came into a lot of money; some loaded distant relation had singled his sorry ass out for the lot. Lucky bastard. Never really worked a day in his life. Brought me up in poverty, but now the Lord has provided. Fuck off. Someone died; you got lucky, old man.

If there is a God, why did he let me grow up in that shit hole? If there is a God, why didn't he protect me from the Devil? There is no God, or if there is, he is a pussy. How dumb was I, right?

Dumb didn't even cover it.

Dad moved us into a secluded farmhouse in the middle of nowhere. He fancied himself as "Lord of the Manor." More like "King of the Shit Pile." There wasn't a church for miles, and dad couldn't drive thanks to the accident he had years ago but won't talk about. So, we were isolated, no church to cleanse my soul. Like I gave a shit. I was coming up on eighteen and would be out of there as soon as I got the chance.

Life is a fickle bastard, always changing its mind on you. I was all set to leave, with bags packed and ready to go. But the night before my birthday, Lucifer came to me again.

"Soon you will be mine, child."

I don't know if it was the crack I had smoked or the gin I had gotten out of the cabinet earlier. All I knew was that I had downed half the bottle. But for the first time, my dark knight lost his beauty for a split second. I saw his true face with the pockmarked, blackened skin, the blood red eyes. He was not the tall dark knight; it was a shrunken, twisted creature, and I was shit-scared.

Later, I was back at the drink cabinet looking for something stronger than gin. I couldn't shake the image of Lucifer from my mind. The Devil was real, and he visited me now even while I was awake. I found my dad in the sitting room, beer bottles scattered about his feet. The music system was on and some miserable country shit was playing. Rolling my eyes, I headed for the hard stuff.

"I loved her you know."

My dad never spoke to me these days. His speech was slurred, and as I turned to look at the wanker who gifted me half of his DNA, I saw the tears in his eyes.

Fuck.

I was not ready for tears. I mumbled something, grabbed the first bottle I came to without reading what it was, and headed back the way I had come.

"You don't understand, Mia, I loved your mother. I didn't mean for her to die."

Did he just tell me? What the fuck?

"I think you need to go to bed," I said, my back still to him. I needed to leave; the guy was havering shit, and I did not need to hear it. Not tonight.

"I killed her, I killed her and now she is haunting me."

A line had just been crossed. Was he actually telling me he murdered my mother? Because that is fucked up. I waited for him to say more. I didn't have to wait long; the words were tumbling out of him.

"I had been drinking, and your mum said she wanted to go home to get to you. She missed you."

The revelations just kept on coming. My would-be lover is actually the Devil, and my dad is telling me not only did he murder my mother, but that she held me when

I was small. She had missed me and wanted nothing more than to be with me.

"I had convinced her to come out. Just for a couple of drinks. You were a good baby, and we knew the sitter would take good care of you. It was while I was driving back home that she told me she was leaving me."

His voice was suddenly hard. The tears forgotten. "She had met a man she loved and wanted to leave. "And to cap it all, you were the cuckoo in my nest. The fucker she loved was your dad, not me."

I felt the room tilt. This man before me was not my father. I was not related to this useless asshole, who beat me and starved me all my short life? He should have shut up then. But he kept going. On and on about how my mother was a whore and that when he pulled to the side of the road that night and chased her into some bushes that she deserved it. She had broken his heart and made him bring up another man's bastard. She was HIS wife and he owned her, 'til death they did part.

"You're a monster; you killed her in some bushes at the side of the road because she didn't love you? Are you insane?"

The weight of the bottle in my hand felt good. He needed to shut up, and I needed to leave. I turned back to the door and almost made it into the hall when I heard him start again.

"I took her body to the fucker's place of work, hid her in his old pickup that he always left there at the weekend. He wouldn't want her anymore after I smashed her pretty face in with a rock."

I don't remember crossing the room or smashing the bottle in my hand on the dresser as I passed it. I do remember the look of horror in his eyes when I stuck the broken neck into his fat belly. I remember plunging it in over and over again until his middle looked like mince. He clung to life though, the evil fucker. Laughing in my face, telling me that my real father was in prison for the murder of my whore of a mother, and he was never going to tell me his name.

It was then I started lacerating his face. I must have sliced him a thousand times. After, when my breathing came hard and the broken bottle was lodged in his left eye socket, I realised what I had done. I was a murderer.

I emptied his wallet and the safe that night. I changed my clothes and grabbed my bag. I was out of there. The Devil might be after my soul, but at least he was honest about it.

I looked for my dad in old newspaper articles on the net, and I even went to the archives. Eventually I found him: Adam Everson. The irony was not lost on me. Lucifer was tormenting my dreams, and my birth father was named Adam—you couldn't make this shit up. I contacted the prison where he was being held. They asked me if I was a relative, and I told them I was his daughter. They took a bit of convincing, but after I agreed to meet the warden they seemed to relax. My meeting was the next day. I used some cash to buy a cheap moped and was there in under an hour. The warden had me taken to his office, where I was offered tea and cookies. I took the cookies.

"Ms. Everson, your father was a first-class inmate. Never had a problem with him, and all the staff respected him. There were some who believed he was innocent . . ."

"Hold up, why are we talking in the past tense here?" I saw Lucifer out of the corner of my eye smiling his beautiful smile. But I knew what was under the mask he wore.

"Adam killed himself two days ago. We found him in his cell."

My mind went blank. My real father was dead. I caught the odd phrase from the warden as I battled for control. Razor, slit wrists, too much blood. Nothing to be done. The ringing in my ears was too loud now; I couldn't hear him any longer. My last connection to a woman I have wanted to know all my life is dead.

"You should not have tried to find redemption here, sweet one." Lucifer was standing before me now. His smile was wide.

He did this.

It had always been him, whispering in my ear. The murder of my stepfather—that was his influence. I'd bet money on it. I looked up into his blue eyes; the answers were there for me to see.

It was months of mental torment that drove me to hack off my own hand. I had killed many, I was told later. I remember looking at the bloody stump and thinking fuck you, Lucifer. He didn't come to me then. I almost bled to death that night. Once I was caught and put in prison, they seemed to think it was normal to cut off your own hand. No psych evaluation for me. I got ahold of whatever I could. Razor blades, shanks, anything I could use to mutilate my perfect white skin. If I was to be Lucifer's bride, I might as well look as gross as he does.

It was the night before they were moving me to the secure hospital that Lucifer returned to me. He laughed in my face and told me that every bad thing that had ever happened to me was because of him. I had been meant for so much more, including a husband and children, a loving home, and a long life. I was his example. I was his gift to his father, to prove that any human can be corrupted, and the consequences would ripple throughout generations.

I asked him through my tears if he had ever wanted me. He laughed in my scarred face and told me that I was scum, all humans were. I was a toy, and now I was broken; he had no more need for me.

"But rest assured, you will be seeing me again. Your place in hell has been reserved since your conception."

They tell me I screamed until I ruptured something in my throat. I am mute now and always bound in restraints. Do I want to die? Yes, so I can stop feeling this pain. I mourn the life that could have been. But I am also so scared; when my time does come, I know the Devil himself will be waiting for me, and my torture will be eternal.

ATTACK OF THE MUNCHIES

BASED ON SLEEPING BEAUTY

There was no way to stop the insatiable hunger. You can't kill people and expect no one to notice. They say you should never run from your problems, that everyone should accept you as you are, including your flaws. This all sounds lovely if it were put into practice hundred percent of the time. However, when you find out your daughter is not quite normal, and the whole acceptance umbrella doesn't cover her particular quirk—life gets real, *really* fast!

That's exactly what happened to Amber; she was born into royalty, betrothed to a prince, and should have had a charmed life. Unfortunately, at a young age Amber started to change. She was unable to even consider eating cooked food, especially vegetables. Most think this is normal for a child, and they'd be correct. Most children go through a period of hating anything that looks remotely healthy or green. However, Amber took this a little too far. She also refused to eat any meat that had been cooked; this included fish. Her parents were embarrassed to have her at the dinner table as they watched her devour plates of raw chicken or her absolute favourite, bloody, raw steaks.

Amber saw absolutely nothing wrong with the way she liked to enjoy her foods. After all, one of her cousins was vegan, and there was nothing as far as she was concerned that was weirder than a person who only wanted and actively enjoyed eating greens.

As she got older, she was invited to less of the family banquets and the huge lavish balls that were held periodically throughout the year. She became depressed; there was no one like her as far as she knew. It was halfway through summer when she noticed that the raw meats were not as satisfying as they once were.

This posed a huge problem; if she couldn't eat meat and she knew she couldn't digest vegetables, how was she meant to survive?

She took her concern to her mother and father in the hope that they would have a plan; maybe a doctor or a mystic could cure her of this affliction. The king and queen looked at their daughter with sad eyes and explained to her that there was no cure for what she suffered from.

This sent Amber into a grave depression. She hardly left her room; she didn't eat for weeks and slowly she began to desiccate. Soon it was too painful to even blink. So, as the first leaves began to turn golden at their edges, signalling the start of autumn, Amber slipped into a coma.

The kingdom went into a deep mourning for their princess. Offerings were left on the castle steps, and every mystic, holy person, and wise woman from miles around came to the princess in the hope that they might cure her and restore her to the people that love her so.

Queen Harriet would sit with her daughter day after day and read to her; she knew that Amber would be well one day. Maybe not in her lifetime, but there was just something about the way her daughter's hair continued to grow thick and strong, and when she touched Amber's paper thin skin it was still warm, the life force still strong within her.

In her comatose state akin to death, it appeared that Amber was completely disconnected to the word. However, she heard, smelt, and felt everything. It was as if she were in hibernation, waiting for something miraculous to take place within herself so that she could awaken. This gave her hope as it meant that there was something better waiting on the other side of this imprisonment of her mind; there had to be. Nobody deserved to be entrapped in a withering husk until the day they truly died.

Still the seasons changed, and the years rolled by. The king died three years after Amber's slip into nothingness. She felt the pain acutely. She had missed her chance to say goodbye to her beloved Papa, and there was no way to gain that time back. Despite crippling grief, her darling mother visited her chamber every day and read to her. Amber could hear the tremor in the queen's voice as she read the book containing her favourite poems and short stories. It was as spring changed to summer of the following year that Amber realised it had been weeks since her mother had read to her. Another week passed or maybe it was two? She was now becoming concerned for her mother's well-being. She had never missed a day visiting, and Amber missed her terribly.

It was incredibly lonely in her room. She couldn't blame them really, out of sight out of mind. It had been years since the last physician had visited and told her beloved parents that she would never wake up. It was then she realised that it was likely that news that had caused her father's untimely death. She knew they had experienced much loss before she was born. So many failed pregnancies, with babies too weak to cling to this earthly plane. No parent wants to outlive their children, and the king and queen had had so many die that once Amber became comatose it broke their hearts.

Then tragedy struck again. Although for Amber it was a miracle, and it happened on a frosty day in midwinter. There still had been no sign of her lady mother for a very long time. She heard the servants taking about their dear Queen Harriet and how she ailed in her chambers, how the people missed her and wondered if she too was to die? Leaving Amber an orphan.

It hurt her deeply that her mother was so sick and that they thought of her as some kind of freak—the corpse in the tower rooms. Some kind of sick caricature of death made flesh, everlasting, never changing. Not dead but not fully alive. She knew from her maid's chatter when they came to tidy her room and change the sheets, that the entire kingdom believed her to be cursed.

It was one of these visits from the maids that changed her existence forever. It was as the sheets were being replaced and new flowers, roses to be exact, were being placed around her head. They had taken to placing flowers around her body. She was aware of her oder; the flowers didn't help hide it. The sweet smell of corruption was inescapable.

The maid, Jodie, she would always remember her name, had been the one arranging the flowers that day when she cut herself. She had carelessly slashed her finger on a thorn while trying to rush the job. Amber understood why she had been trying to hurry, who wanted to hang around a corpse-like princess who breathed foul breath and whose eyelids still moved as the eyes beneath quivered.

Unfortunately for Jodie, the second Amber caught the scent of her blood something deep within her ignited. With speed she didn't know she possessed, Amber grabbed the careless maid, her eyes still closed, sealed shut from lack of use, and pulled Jodie across her frail body. She bit down hard on the first area of bare flesh she could reach.

Jodie's screams were the worst sound that Amber had ever heard and believed she would ever hear in her entire life. She felt great remorse for what she had done. Attacking her maid and eating her alive was not something she was proud of. Yet, it had saved her life. Within moments of consuming human flesh, she began to regenerate. Of course, Margaret, Jodie's companion, had fled screaming for help, that the possessed princess had murdered a royal maid. Amber knew that remaining in her room would mean death. Or would it? Could she actually die? She thought about it and didn't think she could. She had lain in her bed for almost a decade and was still alive. So maybe they would imprison her if they found her there? The thought of existing for another decade as she had been was abhorrent. So, with the strength she had regained from Jodie's sacrifice, she dressed in the most sensible clothes she could find, which sadly were Jodie's. All her own clothes were far too small; they were the clothes of her girlhood, and now she was a woman grown.

She had just finished dressing, when the sound of a commotion could be heard, and it was getting closer to her bedroom door every second. There was nowhere to run; she had to either face them and hope she escaped the cells later or take her chances by jumping out the window. Amber knew that her room was in the tower; the tower was at least twenty feet high and below were jagged rocks and the fast-flowing water of the Oom River. Even in her altered state, she didn't relish the idea of facing that kind of fall. If she survived it at all. Her mortality was still in question after all.

Suddenly the choice was taken from her as the door flew open and two palace guards stood before her. She was a bit affronted that they had only sent two and that her mother was not with them. Then again, maybe the news that her only child had just ripped the face off her maid might not have been the best way to announce Amber's return from near death.

Thankfully, the guards were so shocked to see the princess on her feet and looking relativity normal that they paused just long enough to allow Amber to push past them and run as fast as her legs could carry her, down the tower stairs, along the corridor, and out into the palace grounds.

There was nowhere to run in the gardens, one side was the river and on the other was the great wall that separated the castle from the rest of the kingdom. There was no way she could stay within the walls; they would find her and surely try to do her harm. Understandable, just not something she really wanted to experience in the near future. It was then that she felt an agonising hunger. A hunger that was new and yet even though the compulsion was strong, Amber tried to resist it. She wasn't a killer, not in her heart anyway. The problem was that once she had had her first taste of warm living flesh, human flesh and lapped at the blood, there was going to be a next time. She could feel it as surely as night follows the day.

It was as she ran to the greenhouse, knowing that she could scale the wall by using one of the trees that grew nearby, that she was grabbed and tossed to the ground. Snarling, she sprang to her feet and turned to face her attacker.

She stopped and stared.

She knew this man; he had been a boy when she had last seen him, and he had called her a brat and pulled her pigtails. It was William, her betrothed. Horror froze his handsome face as he took in Amber's blood-stained appearance and milky eyes. He knew she was the princess and his intended, but she was truly terrifying.

He drew his short sword and prepared for her attack. It was Amber who backed off; she had no desire to hurt him. That was a lie; she wanted to eat his warm insides and wash them down with his blood. Yet this was William, her William, and there was no way she would steal the heir of her ally's kingdom just because she had an attack of the munchies and was half crazed with a fever.

She really wouldn't have attacked him, only he stuck his sword in her left side as she turned to flee. Something inside her snapped. She became this other creature, feral, predatory, and absolutely lethal. William didn't stand a chance.

Within seconds, his sword was lost in the grass, meters away, and his would-be wife was on him; her once beautiful hands were more like claws as they ripped at his shirt and tore into his flesh. Lord forgive him, he punched her in the side of the jaw, hoping it would knock her out and he could then restrain her somehow. The blow only seemed to anger her, and with a sound that no human should be able to make, Amber brought back her right fist and punched a hole clean through his ribs and grabbed his frantically beating heart.

Amber was enthralled; the feel of his heart still pumping delicious blood was intoxicating. For a second, the mist cleared from her fevered mind and she became Amber again. She looked into William's pale face and his deep blue eyes and only saw hatred there. It hurt her even though she knew that she was the sole cause of it.

He used her momentary lack of attention to punch her hard in the face again. This time she felt something shift, and when she heard his scream and felt the wetness run off her chin, she felt the rage return. Amber looked at his hand and saw that a large part of her face clung to his fist like a wet rag. Without thinking, she squeezed his palpitating organ, and all the while she looked into this wide blue eyes. Undeterred, she ripped out his heart. William had enough time to register the missing organ, so vital to live, and watched as Princess Amber took a bite out of his still quivering flesh. Her lipless mouth closing around his heart was the image he took to his grave.

SETTING THE RECORD STRAIGHT

BASED ON PUSS IN BOOTS

Everyone knows the story of Puss in Boots, how the cat was a mastermind and managed to make a poor boy a prince . . . But that's how the humans tell it. I am going to tell you my story. I warn you it is a sad one of kidnap and servitude.

So, if you are sitting comfortably, I will begin.

I WAS TAKEN from my mother at a young age, maybe eight weeks old. I was the runt, you see, and my siblings pushed me out. Being small was not all bad. It made hiding from the giants—who I later learned to be humans—easier. They would come to the barn and handle us in turn, and one-by-one my brothers and sisters left. My mother had a serious dislike for me, and I never knew my father. The day my last sibling went with yet another human, she left too. You read it correctly: My own mother abandoned me in a cold and smelly barn.

It was three days later that I managed to find a hole in the barn wall and escape. It was short lived. I was discovered by the humans. They picked me up and poked at my tiny belly and muttered about throwing the "hairball" in the river.

They meant me!

Well, I was not having it. I bit the hand that held me and ran as fast as my tiny legs would go. *How would I survive?* I did not know. All I wanted was to be away from humans and their harsh words and grabbing hands.

Six months of being my own cat was wonderful. I travelled the land and ate as many mice as I could catch. Life was grand. Then, I got caught again. This time was worse: It was a dog that caught me. That great big slobbering thing got my coat all wet. I was not at all happy. I was carried back to a huge building.

A portly man was just coming out of the door to one of the outbuildings, when he spotted me in the dog's mouth. He told the foul beast to "drop it."

Wonderful, I would be the "it."

Thud!

This incident began my new life as a working mouser in a smelly mill. The miller had three children; mercifully, they ignored me mostly. Apart from the girl—yes, the human tale says it was a boy child I helped but that is not true—who loved to hunt me out.

"Here, Puss Puss. Where are you?"

Those words instilled real fear in my heart. It meant Lydia wanted to play Puss in Boots—which meant I needed to hide. Puss in Boots was what the charming devil's spawn called dressing me up in her dolls' clothes. It was degrading and very uncomfortable. I never evaded her for long. Lydia was small and very agile, so she always found my best hiding spots. I think having two older brothers didn't help much. The mill was pretty remote, and Lydia had no friends to speak of. I wanted to help, I really did, just not by wearing her bloody dolls' get-up for a start. I'm a boy, and also, I have a tail.

This torture went on for years. As I grew, so did she, and she always found a way to dress me up. Finding her old baby clothes was her first option once I became too big for the dolls' clothes. There are a lot of mice in a grain mill, and the only way I didn't get locked in the coal bunker was by doing my "job." I tried to run away. Lord, how I tried. But Lydia always found me, and the collar with the stupid bell on it did not help any escape plan either.

SKIP FORWARD A FEW MISERABLE YEARS . . .

THE MILL WAS NOT PRODUCING as much, and Lydia's papa was dying. Her brothers were fighting over who gets what when the old man kicks the bucket. All I wanted to do was sleep. With the grain stores that were almost depleted, there wasn't much work for me to do and not a lot of food either. I just wanted some peace and quiet.

Ultimately, Lydia's papa died in his bed. I was all for packing up my troubles and hightailing it out of there, until I heard the brothers' plan. They were going to sell Lydia as part of the sale of the mill. Now, this child had been the bane of my life for years, but she had never hurt me or chased me. Not like her piggy-eyed brothers. So right then, I decided to stay with her. I know, I know, I said it was a horrible tale and it is. Imagine being abandoned and then having to escape death only to wind up a slave. Not exactly a fairytale, is it?

The mill was sold, and Lydia and I stayed on. She was

a girl of fifteen by then, and I was getting on a bit. I was lucky—for once—the new owner had brought traps with him, so I was able to get the mice without the hard work. My knees were not what they once were. So, we plodded on, Lydia and I, for what seemed like forever. She had finally stopped dressing me up, and I took to sleeping in her room.

After a hard winter, the new miller couldn't afford to keep Lydia any longer, and after giving her three silver coins and a sack for her belongings, she was put on the back of the miller's cart and taken into the town. I went with her, of course. I felt like I should be there for her, plus it was only a matter of time before the guy kicked me out too. It was awful to listen to her cry as we stood alone in the darkening town square. For the first time in my life, I was free, and yet I was actively choosing to remain with a human.

It wasn't until the next day that we made our way to the tailor's shop. Lydia had been making me clothes for years and for herself, so she thought she would try the tailor. I was in the sack keeping warm and wishing she had made me a jumper. I know, I didn't want to be a Puss in Boots, but I was getting old, and the cold and old bones do not make for a happy cat.

Thankfully, the tailor, a young man by the name of John, was willing to hire Lydia. I wasn't fooled: He thought she was pretty. So, we moved into John's spare room above the tailor shop. Lydia loved her work, and I loved the coal fire in the parlour. That was where they found me you know, by the fire, curled up inside one of John's boots. So right at the very end I was, indeed, a true Puss in Boots.

See . . . Sad . . .

Go ahead and shed a tear for the old cat who found out in his winter years that some humans are okay. I sit in cat heaven now, watching Lydia and John fuss over their children and the kittens they stopped a man from throwing in the river. Sometimes I wish I could go back down to earth and lie by the fire again. Then I remember what it's like to be grabbed by sticky hands.

No thank you!

So now you know, there was no princess or trolls. (Really! You humans and your imaginations.) The only part that was true was that there was a happy ever after for us all.

And you just read a story written by a cat. Who's crazy now?

CONCRETE CHILD

BASED ON PINOCCHIO

JUNE 1950

I wish I could feel like a real boy, not this broken thing. The pity and the stares are becoming too much. It must be joyous to play in the sunshine and run free with the wind catching your hair. I wouldn't know such things. My life is spent in this chair with my chest and thighs held still by thick leather straps. My useless arms folded in my lap. I can feel the drool sliding from the corner of my mouth; it takes its time, sliding down my sore chin and dripping with a pat onto my shirt. Mother will be with my sister Elisa. My nurse has gone for her lunch. I hate that woman; she speaks to me like my wits are as broken as my body. I suppose I can't place the blame there, after all, I can't verbalise my needs and wants. I am trapped in this broken body that my mind I cannot escape.

NICK SAT and looked out the window. The summer sun beat against his pale face. To be eleven and forever trapped in his chair was one thing. But to be forgotten for seemingly longer periods was really getting to him.

Why should I be left alone while the family plays and eats together? I say the family because I do not feel a part of that togetherness. They are the walkers, and I am the freak they hide from the world. Nick the concrete child. I hear them, the physicians. My illness has a name: fibrodysplasia ossificans. They say that it is progressive. I don't know what it means, just that I can't really move. I am more stone than wooden, I guess. The children that come and play with Elisa call me Pinocchio. It hurts because I can't fight back. Sometimes they come in and move my arms. It hurts so much. But I can't tell them to stop.

Days turn into weeks and Nick gets worse. A fall from his bed breaks his right arm, and it calcifies at an odd angle. His father can't even look at him. His only son, a simple-minded cripple. If only he knew what was going on inside Nick's head—the stories he creates and the dreams he has every night. But no one cares about the concrete child, shut away in his room.

July 1950

I have a new doctor. He is a stern gentleman with a love for smoking his pipe and wearing tweed. He says that he has an idea to test my cognitive abilities and that it won't hurt. Everything hurts, but I see the hope in my mother's eyes and decide to endure it. If she could just see that I am in here, maybe I would become real to her. The real boy she always wanted to have.

The doctor is a moron. His great idea was to get me to blink at cards he held up. "Once for yes" and "twice for no." Well, it didn't go well. He clearly forgot the rules after the fourth card because he became cross and declared me an imbecile and not worth his time. The look of disappointment on my father's face was expected. My mother, on the other hand, ordered Dr. Lewis to leave that very moment. Father just shook his head and left the room. I felt the tears as they built in the corners of my eyes. I wanted to scream at them all.

"I am here! I am not stupid, and I can hear you!"

The feeling of complete despair was too much. I closed my eyes on the harsh world and hoped to fall into Dreamland. The sand felt warm and dry between his toes; the breeze was fresh and the sky a bright blue. Nick loved to visit the beach in Dreamland. It never rained, and there were always children to play with. Football was his favourite game. The other children had taught him the rules. Cassy was his best friend in Dreamland. In the real world, she had cerebral palsy and was likely to die in the next two years.

I told her I was sorry. As hard as my life as the concrete child was, death was still scary. The ultimate unknown. Cassy would laugh at me and punch my shoulder. "No, Silly, death is the only true adventure. We can then be free," she would always say. I'd smile and mess her hair before running off toward the shoreline. I love to run. It is the best feeling in the world. My toes are buried in the wet sand, the gentle waves lapping at my ankles.

"Nick."

"Nicolas, sweetheart, wake up for mother, darling, wake up."

I am ripped from the shore and Cassy by my mother

gently shaking me. The pain that rips through me even with such a gentle touch causes me to open my mouth in a silent scream.

"I know you understand me. You are not stupid, do you hear me, darling Nick? I know you are in there."

The sliver of hope that I have always held onto begins to grow. She believes me. I want to wrap my arms around her and tell her I love her. That I forgive her for forgetting me up here. But I can't of course, so I raise my eyebrows and wait.

"Yes, Darling, I know you are trapped in there. I watch you while you sleep. You smile and your hands move. I won't give up on you. Please believe that."

Tears well in my almond eyes again as I look at the woman who brought my broken body into the world. Her tears reflect my own in her brilliant green eyes. For the first time in what feels like forever, my mother leans forward and kisses me. It feels like coming home.

August

CASSY SAYS she is spending more time in Dreamland; she says her body is so sick right now that this is the only place she can be happy. It scares me because this will happen to me at some point. My illness is progressive; I know what that means now. Life-limiting and increasingly painful. But I don't want to die. I know Dreamland is not where we go when we die. No one knows where that even is because none of the children can come back here. The unknown scares me more than the pain.

Father has stopped coming to visit me in my room. Mother tells me it's because it's too hard for him. I know it's because he is disgusted with me. I hear them fight. He wants to put me in the hospital. I stopped respecting my father a while ago. It makes the heartbreak less painful. Mother comes every day. She has even taken to feeding me my meals. Father won't allow me in the dining room, so she brings a meal to my room. I try hard not to make a mess. She doesn't seem to mind and talks to me throughout the meal, even pauses to allow me to make any expressions I am able to. It gives me hope. She hears me even though I cannot speak. She sits with me sometimes, until I wander off into dreams.

Dreamland is always sunny, but I want to feel rain on my face. The other children get super cross when I wish for rain, but tonight I am strangely alone here. The thunder rips though the sky as I walk along the beach. It is an awesome display of power. I imagine I am the lightning rushing across the sky. I am powerful and so alive. The next thing I know, I am running on the clouds. The world below is beautiful and so far away. Suddenly, I am scared. I don't want to be disconnected from the earth. That is my home, my safety net, and my anchor. Panic shoots through me like the lightning. And I scream. The sound is alien to me; I have never screamed. Not even in Dreamland.

The real world rushes back at me. Dreamland is gone. But something is very wrong. I am shaking all over, and I can't stop. The pain is unreal, and the fear is blinding. Mother is there with a few others. Ambulance crew, I think. There is a lot of talking, but I can't focus. I don't want to die. I look for my mother. She is there looking at me with a fear I never wanted to see. This is bad. This could be my end.

October

Today I woke up, I was in Dreamland for a really long time. Cassy was there but she left from time to time. I didn't. The night I had the seizure was the same night I went into a coma. I remember my mother saying to me when I finally stopped fitting that she loved me and that I would be okay. I didn't feel okay. The world was fuzzy, and my mouth was dry with something stuck in my throat. I was too drowsy to panic. My head would not move at all. I could tell that it was night, so I allowed the drowsy feeling to claim me again. Dreamland is better than being in that bed alone and scared. Cassy is waiting for me. She looks sad, which is unnerving because no one is sad here. Ever.

"I am sorry, Nick," she says before throwing her arms around me. I look confused and she then hits me with a truth I already knew. I am dying. It turns out our parents attend a "coping together" support group, and she heard her mother mention me by name. The seizure had caused massive cerebral damage. I wasn't expected to last the

week. I tell her I just woke up in the real world though, so that couldn't be right. Her tears are the only answer I get. At least she's tried to be honest with me.

November

I HELD on for a full month. No one was telling me when I was going to die. I spent the night, and anytime I was not with mother, in Dreamland. I wrote letters to her in Dreamland. I always signed them from her concrete child. They contained memories and answers to all the questions she ever wondered about. It seemed the closer I got to death, the clearer everything became. I no longer feared what was to come. I would be a real boy in every way.

I saw Cassy one last time before I died. She was so sad. It was hard to see her sad. I asked her to get a message to my mother for me if she could. I wanted to make sure that mother knew I was ok.

December

MRS WALKER LOOKED out at the few people who had come to lay her beautiful boy to rest. The night of the seizure would haunt her always . She was forever thankful that Nicolas had woken up a few times just to be with her. She felt he was in there, her boy, her concrete child, her Pinocchio. She knew how he hated the nickname Elisa's friends had given him and how it had hurt him. To her, he was that fictional wooden boy full of love and adventure. Now he was free from his broken shell. He could be a real-life boy, and although she missed him, the thought of his freedom from pain was a relief.

Looking at the tributes that had come from the hospital and far flung relatives, who for the most part had refused Nick's existence, she took no notice of those over- the-top wreaths and messages. They were notes of guilt, not of love. The last posy was small and shaped like a football. She just knew that it was special. Bending to pick it up, she saw the card attached, it was addressed to Mother. With her heart in her mouth, Mrs. Walker opened the small card:

Mother,

Do not be sad for me. I am happy, and I am grateful to you. The concrete child is no more. I am free now. Be happy for me, Mother. I love you and wish I could have told you. But like you always said, you knew I was in there. My favourite colour is green. I really liked your songs and the banana cake you used to blend for me with cream. I'll never forget the smell of your hair. Rain was always my favourite thing to listen to.

I loved you all my life with all my heart.

Nick

SKINNER

BASED ON RUMPLSTILTSKIN

Skin. It's a funny old thing. It keeps your insides in and your outside looking pretty. It comes in all colours. If you beat it hard enough, it even goes purple, green, and blue. I am a collector of skin. It's how I punish those who don't settle up at the end of our arrangement. I'm a nice man, polite and well dressed. I offer fair terms, and all I ask is that you pay your dues when the job is done. People tell their kiddies bedtime stories about me.

"Better behave, child, or Robbie will come and steal your skin."

It's a bit over the top; I'd never hurt a bairn. I had one once, a bairn I mean. She was the bonniest thing I ever did see. But her mother, well, let's just say that was the only time I got skinned, for nothing more than asking her to marry me. I carry the scar of that proposal for all to see. The ugly melted skin on my cheek is the physical reminder of the day she took my baby and ripped my heart out. I have been searching for them ever since. I will be paid my due.

I HAVE RUN FAR and the child is hungry, but the gold in my pockets will keep us fed for a while. The day my plan came crashing down, was the day that stupid bastard asked me to marry him. Like I would. He is no one, just a man with no future.

One day he might catch me, but for now we run. I should have known better than to steal from him; I knew how much he respected me and would have given me and his child the world. But I am wrong in some way; something essential is missing within me, and I wasn't prepared to stay and curse him too. I feel bad about his handsome face. His scream will haunt me till my last breath. The child is sleeping, thankfully, and the moon is full; I can run all night if I have to. I need as much distance between me and Robert as possible.

SHE'S BEEN THROUGH HERE, I know she has, my dog knows her scent. Carrie should have left my child; that's all I wanted, my beautiful baby girl. We had not yet named her. But I have one in mind now. The road that she has taken leads to the next town; it has a station. If she boards a train I will lose them, and I can't be without my child. The murderous things I want to do to Carrie Idare not give voice to now. She made me the monster I have become.

I didn't mean to kill the whore the other night; she just wouldn't leave me be. I was on my way home from the pub, dulling the pain as usual, when this doxy appeared and wanted to warm my bed for a few quid. I told her politely the first time that I was not looking for a woman tonight or any night. The silly cow followed me regardless.

"Piss off. I do not want a doxy to follow me home; you

won't get a penny off me so go look for business elsewhere."

I know I was a bit harsh with my language, but she would not bugger off. I bet she wanted the money to score later. She followed me all the way to my house. Came in behind me. I could have stopped her, but by then I was already past the point of no return. Her hair was the same shade as Carrie's, and they wore the same perfume. It was all too much.

I had never killed anything before. I feel like I missed a few steps in the serial killer evolution. There she was, pinned under me, her eyes and tongue bulging, as I choked the life from her. The movies make it look easy. It's bloody not. You have to maintain the grip for ages. My hand was getting sore, and I really thought the bitch would never die.

After, when I sat on the floor next to her, I felt a mixture of emotions. There was shame for sure, I had raised my hand to a woman, horror at the fact I had a dead one in my hall, and euphoria. I felt powerful and justified. She had come into my home after I told her to piss off. She had it coming. She should be glad I hadn't raped her first.

I wish I could say I stopped there. I wish I had just left her body in the fire escape stairway and let the police deal with another "wasted life." But something happened to me that night. The rage and hurt churned inside me and morphed into something far worse, a calm detachment that led me to take my cut-throat razor to her flesh and ever so carefully render skin from bone.

~

THE NEXT TOWN WAS BIGGER; I knew we needed to find somewhere to stay. My unnamed daughter was cold, and I was so worried that she would die if I did not find us somewhere permanent to stay. I was loath to let people know we had money. A lone woman and a baby would be easy pickings for the local pimp and those whose greed outweighed their morals.

I stopped for a moment outside a townhouse, its Edwardian facade imposing in its grandeur. This is the sort of place my child deserved to live. She should be treated as a princess. As tiny as she is, I knew she would have hair the colour of gold thread and eyes as blue as the sky. Blue like her father's.

I heard the front door open and went to move on, but whoever it was called to me. It was a woman. I looked over at her; she was the housekeeper maybe. It was hard to tell; the path to the door was long, and the light that shone behind her hid her from view. She walked down the path and begged me to come inside. She had heard the baby crying, and Mr. Lewis, the owner of the house, was away on business and would not mind. He loved children. With no other choice really, I let the woman usher me and my daughter into the house.

~

I HAD KILLED along the road searching for Carrie, so many faceless people. I carried pieces of them with me, panels of skin that I had stitched together and wore under my shirt, with a bucket of aftershave to mask the stench.

Now I was close; I could feel it. The bloody dog had had us thrown off the bus for pissing, so I had been walking for a good few miles. The dog was long gone. I shouted at him and he ran off. I'd have done the same had I watched my master kill and skin his own kind without blinking.

It wouldn't be long until I sniffed her out. All the money she had taken, it was all marked. The police had been informed not an hour past. The second she spent some, it was all over.

I fantasied about skinning her. Alive. How long would it be before her nerves were overloaded and she had a heart attack? I hope it is a while. She ripped out my heart taking my baby. This was her karma. Was I a monster now? Probably. I don't really care. I have a goal and my code. I want my daughter, and I will have my due.

~

PHEOBE WAS SO good to us. She was great with Rose; that's the name I had finally given my daughter. She was thriving, and for a moment I dared to dream that we would never be found by Robert. It had been four days; he should have passed through here by now, I hope. But the ball of fear in my stomach would not shift. I shouldn't have burnt him. He was a handsome man, and I had taken even that from him. I couldn't tell him the truth though; he would have wanted to help me, and that would have got him killed. This was for the best.

I had to head out today. Cabin fever was taking root, and Rose needed some nappy cream. Phoebe said she would go, but I asked if she would watch the baby instead. I had not been anywhere without my child since her birth, and to walk without her in my arms for half an hour would be a tiny moment to be just Carrie.

~

I KNEW she would come out of her hole sooner or later. I had been staying, as it happened, in the hotel opposite the house she was staying in. Bitch had landed on her feet, judging by the fancy pile she just walked out of. At least my daughter was safe. My heart stopped, where was she? Carrie had no child with her. The rage was building. If that bitch had hurt or given up my child, skinning her would be the very least of her worries.

How lucky I had been to be standing at the window that morning with my coffee. I would have missed her had I been a few moments longer in the bath. Fate was clearly on my side. I watched as she headed toward the centre of town; it was only two streets away. I dashed about, getting dressed and checked my pocket for my blade. It was time to go hunting.

It was easy to find her. Her masses of golden hair shone like a beacon. I followed her around a few shops. She stopped in the pharmacy and bought nappies and cream. Thank God, my child was alive, and I knew exactly where to find her. Once I was done with Carrie, I was going to get my child. I let her enjoy the last moments of freedom before I drew up beside her outside the baker's.

"If you scream, I will gut you here and now," I said to her with my blade pressing against the exposed skin on her hip. It amazed me how quickly she had got her figure back. Then again, running from the man you just partly melted is bound to burn come calories.

"Robert." *He found me. I should have listened to my gut and kept running. At least I don't have Rose with me.*

"Yes, it's your jilted lover. My face is still fucking sore, thanks for asking."

I gripped her arm and began leading her down the high street. I had already found a place I could use. It was quiet and no longer used. Best of all it was underground.

She screamed for an age, and the blood went everywhere. I loved every second of it. I am proud of myself and my new personal record; I managed to flay half of her before she died. It wasn't so much fun then, so I was less precise. I had planned ahead and bought a large bag. Plus, a huge zip lock bag and some preserving fluid. I intended to tan her hide and use it as a door mat. It's all she is good for.

The woman at the house, well, she got in my way. All I wanted was my daughter. My little Grace. That is the name I had given her on my journey to find her. The owner was going to come home to a right mess. Not my problem. I had what I came for, and Carrie had finally paid her due.

I can hear the parents telling their kids the story of "Bad Robbie," the man who steals the skin from naughty children; that's not true. I'd never hurt a child or anyone else that is innocent. But if you take from me, steal from me, or cheat me. I will have my due

GINGERBREAD AND THE W.S.G

BASED ON HANSEL AND GRETEL BY THE BOTHERS GRIMM

Fran was at her bi-weekly support group. It had been fourteen years since she was held for ransom. Fourteen years and she still had nightmares. Tonight, Fran was going to do something she had never done before at this group. She would tell her tale. She arrived at the meeting hall a little before the start time. Taking a deep breath, she checked her bag for her journal and stowed her broom in the allocated spot. The sky was clear tonight and the moon bright. Fran was able to read the notice board that gets put out every two weeks. Her eyes followed the curves of the letters.

W.S.G

MEETING STARTS AT 8PM SHARP. BROOMS TO BE LEFT OUTSIDE. FAMILIARS ARE WELCOME. (BRING POOP- SCOOP AND BAGS PLEASE).

THE LAST PART always made her laugh. They could just magic away the poop. Still, she figured it was in case humans saw the sign. They never made it inside though. The door was charmed so that any human who tried to enter the meeting found themselves back on the street with no memory of how they got there.

Looking up, Fran noticed several group members arriving and decided to head in. She wanted a seat near the door tonight. The idea of a quick exit was very appealing. The stuffy room that always smelled of moth-balls greeted her. Morag, the group leader, was just putting out the wine and oatcakes. It used to be ginger- bread, but the panic it caused to several of the members, including Fran, was too much.

The room was beginning to fill, so Fran quickly took the seat nearest the door as planned. She would have loved some wine to settle her, but it was too late now. There was a no casting rule while in group so that was that. Morag waited for the group to be seated and smiled out at them.

"Blessed be, Sisters," she sang. Fran wanted to throat punch her. Her happiness pissed her off. Of all the witches present, Morag had never lived through a bad human experience.

"Blessed be," came the muttered replies. Unper- turbed by the frosty reception, Morag ploughed on as only she could. Short and rotund with hair that refused to sit flat, she looked more like a fat fairy than a witch.

"Tonight, Fran will be bravely sharing her experience with us. Now, please remember the rules." As if a switch had been flipped, the whole group started to recite the rules of the circle:

"Be kind." "Be honest."

"Be non-judgmental." "Do no harm."

What a load of balls; Fran couldn't stop herself from rolling her eyes. She glanced around; no one seemed to have noticed. Phew. Morag gestured for Fran to enter the centre of the circle and begin in her own time. This is it. *Woman up, Francesca, they can't hurt you anymore.*

"Greetings, sisters. Ermm, tonight . . . I . . ."

Fran froze; she couldn't do this. The memories were still sharp, and the nightmares, oh the nightmares, would she ever be rid of them? *Not if you don't stop being a baby you won't.*

"You know what? I am just going to read from this," she said, holding up her battered journal. Opening it at the first page, Fran began to read:

Mabon

I was getting ready for the festival. I had chosen this year to have a private ritual rather than join the coven. I had not long recovered from the flu and did not wish to pass any lingering sickness to my sisters. I had made some wine earlier in the day and planned to make an offering to the Goddess that evening. First, I must plant the seeds for next spring. Mabon is my most favourite time of the year. I love welcoming back the dark for the winter and the restoration of mother earth before her rebirth in the spring.

The day had been like any other, and I was content. That is, until they came. I had felt their presence in the surrounding woodland before; humans never wandered too close to my home. I meant them no harm, far from it, but I do grow some deadly plants for rituals and so had put up wards to stop anyone coming in and hurting them- selves. They all knew who I was—what I was. But we rubbed along together just fine.

I thought nothing of the children being there that late afternoon. After all, the conkers had begun falling, and they all swarmed the forest like bees, looking for the biggest to take home and soak in vinegar. Nothing works better to make them as tough as stone, unless you know a witch, of course. For the children who lived nearby, I always spelled a couple of buckets. It meant all the children had a chance at owning a strong conker for their games. Silly I know, but I do believe in fairness.

Well, these two particular children were different. Out they came from the woods, a boy and a girl who were the spitting image of one another. I couldn't place them: They must be new to the settlement. I smiled at them and waved and wished them a good evening, safe in the knowledge that they couldn't enter my domain. That's when the boy produced the white oak blade. He made cuts in the fence posts, and the wards I had put up began to fade.

Fran looked up from her book. Her audience was stock still, waiting to hear what happened next. She glanced at Morag and received an encouraging nod.

Taking a breath, she looked back at the words and lost herself within them.

I had no time to cast a new ward; the children were already within the boundary of my home. I did all I could do. I made a dash for my front door. As every good witch knows, you make the outside space a magical null so you cannot be attacked by another witch or magical being. This always seemed safe to me, but it stopped me from removing the two children from my front garden.

They ran after me. I could hear the soft thuds of their leather shoes as they chased me to my door. What did they want with me? I never asked. I just ran. I thought I had made it as I turned and closed the heavy wooden door, sliding the bolts into place. My breath was coming in short, sharp gasps. I needed to relax. I needed to cast new wards. Thankfully, that did not take long.

I found the wine I'd made on the last Mabon and, toasting the Goddess, I had a very long drink. It was as I was pouring a second glass that I saw the children, but not through the window as I expected. I had hoped not to see them at all. But I did, in the refection of my cooking pots that hung on hooks from the rafters.

"By the Goddess!"

The children had found a way in, and now I was close enough to see the whites of their eyes and their milk teeth. I knew these were not ordinary children. They smiled eerily sweet smiles as they approached me. I tried to cast a repelling charm, but nothing happened; these children were nulls!

A collective gasp went up from the group. Fran shuddered; nulls were feared by all magical beings. They stopped any magic from being cast or manifested. A null rendered a witch powerless, no matter how strong or old she was. Swallowing and licking her lips, Fran turned back to the task in hand.

I asked them what they wanted. They just kept coming in slow measured steps. There was nothing for me to do. They had me trapped, and they knew it. Nulls or not I would not harm a child. "DO NO HARM" was all I could hear repeating in my head. The next thing I knew, I was tied to a chair and left in the centre of the room. Still they would not speak to me. The boy kept coming over and cutting me with the white oak blade. The pain was unreal, and I begged him to stop. He just laughed and carried on, cutting my arms, my hands, and my cheeks. I prayed he would not cut my forehead. Damage to my third eye would be permanent.

"Henry, leave the witch. Come and help me. I want to bake something," I heard the girl child say. So, I knew his name now. Not that it helped me, but a connection may help me wear them down and get them to see me as a real person and not just a plaything.

"Shush, Greta! We said we were not going to speak!" Clearly Greta was younger and less worried about being caught. That worried me, too. What did they have planned for me?

"What are you going to make then?" her brother asked, as it was clear for all to see that they were siblings.

"Gingerbread!" she exclaimed, while waving her arms like windmills and knocking my fruit bowl to the floor.

I SAW the pieces of Grandmother's clay bowl skitter across the flagstones. The children set to work stoking my fire and making a fine mess of my kitchen in their quest to make gingerbread. The smell to this day haunts me. I asked for water and had a jug of it poured over my head. I begged for the outhouse to relive myself. They just laughed, and I messed myself after hours of waiting.

The whole house stank of gingerbread. The child had over-sweetened it, and the cloying scent permeated the air and caused me to gag.

"Look, Henry, the hag is hungry, let's feed her some."

I shook my head and clamped my lips shut. It was fresh from the oven. The boy came and pinched my nose closed as the girl advanced on me with scalding hot ginger- bread on the end of the toasting fork.

"Open up, hag, I need to know if it is good,"

The malice in her eyes spoke of a wrongness that went all the way to her core, and I was not fooled. I wanted to scream at them, but opening my mouth would be foolish. The air of my last breath was all but used up. I had to breathe.

The sticky bread burned my mouth. Tears leaked from my eyes, and the children danced around me. Henry cut me with his white oak, and Greta forced more bread into me. It went on for days. They never seemed to tire, and the torture just got worse. They made a syrup with sugar and rose petals from my garden and painted the walls with it and then me. The burns are still visible in some places.

"What stopped them?"

The voice pulled Fran from her memories, and she once again found herself in the hall with the members of the Witches' Support Group.

"Pardon me?"

She caught the eye of Tessa. Tessa had shared the week

before. She had been blamed for the coma of the princess of her kingdom. All untrue of course: The girl had eaten a deadly nightshade, and instead of killing her it had put her to sleep. She would wake one day.

"What stopped the children?" Tessa asked, again, giving Fran an encouraging smile. Fran smiled weakly back.

"Their parents. They were travellers and the children had run off. Their father was furious. He said he knew what they were, and that was why they never stayed in one place for long,"

"But the story we know is that a witch stole the children away," Julie piped up. There was a smirk on her face. Fran hated her.

"True, but witches can't lie, and you all heard my tale. Did it not have the ring of truth?"

They all nodded.

"Humans make up stories to protect their young and to warn those who wish to cause trouble. Those children were the bane of my life for three weeks."

Her voice cracked, and a single tear slid down her flushed cheek.

"Where are they now?" Morag asked while she passed Fran a frilly hankie.

"I don't know. This was years ago. As you know, they will be grown now. I know I never wish to see them again."

OUTSIDE, under the glittering moon. A young man and woman read the sign:

W.S.G

MEETING STARTS AT 8PM SHARP. BROOMS TO BE LEFT OUTSIDE. FAMILIARS ARE WELCOME. (BRING POOP-SCOOP AND BAGS PLEASE).

"Looks like this is the place for us, dear brother."

"Yes, Greta, I believe it is."

KILLER HEELS

BASED ON CINDERELLA

To really understand my story, we will have to go back to the beginning. When my life as I knew it hit the fan. My mother died when I was a young girl, and my father seemed so incapable of living without a woman to warm his slippers and cook his meals, that he married the first one he came across, scarcely a year after losing Mother. My new "step-mum" was called Kira Dutton; she had two daughters, one slightly older than I was and one a year younger than me. I was suddenly the dreaded middle child. Their names were Precious and Divine.

I know the names are laughable, but it was the thing at the time to curse your kids with truly stupid names when they were small, never considering the effect it was going to have on them as grownups. I am lucky my mother named me Ella.

So, the "step-monster" and the gruesome sisters moved into our country pile; I was less than thrilled about this. They were all noisy and rude to the housekeeper. The sisters stole my things, and I would either never see them again or find them weeks later, hidden away in a cupboard and broken.

Dad would just chuckle and tell me that this is what it meant to have siblings. I knew that he just didn't want to end up sleeping in the guest room like the last time he dared to say a word against his stepdaughters. Kira was a hard woman, and Dad was completely spineless when it came to her. I hated it.

We all lived like this for years. As my sisters and I grew to be teenagers, the jealousy really became apparent. I had been blessed with my mother's good looks—thick chestnut hair and green eyes that were slightly cat-like in appearance. Looking at the other two, it made me wonder if their father was even human. They were very hairy and had large noses and piggy eyes that seemed to get lost under thick brows and permanent scowls. Yet their mother, as all mothers should, told them how beautiful they were and bought them the best clothes and shoes money could buy. I also got new (to me) clothes and shoes. Usually cast-offs that were far too big for me. I was glad to be quite skilled with a needle and thread and soon learned how to fashion my own clothes from the sack-like garments gifted to me.

All sounds like a regular blended family, right? Wrong. These people hated me. I was too much like my mother, and Kira hated to be reminded of her. Dad just let her have her way, and as time went on, he grew sick and never seemed to get any better. I resented him then, and I guess I still do to some degree today. He died of a massive heart attack on Christmas day, face first in his goose and gravy. Kira didn't look too surprised; I bet she had been poisoning him for months. There was a small funeral for Dad, and like my mother before him, all memory of his existence was erased from the house and throw out at the earliest opportunity.

Being seventeen and on the streets was not the easiest way to live. Oh yeah, along with my Dad's stuff I was ousted as well. I was pretty, which meant it was easy to make money, but I didn't want to make it that way. My father may have been a spineless fool, but I was my mother's daughter and had slightly more self-respect.

I was lucky enough to get a space in a home as a maid and worked my backside off to please the family. They treated me better than the one who threw me on the street before Dad's body was even cold. So, life seemed to be on the up.

There was to be a huge event in the summer in the biggest nightclub in the city; some European royal was coming to the rebrand opening. The club had been there for years, but after spending an eye-watering amount of money on a total refit and advertising campaign, it was all set to be the place to go and be seen.

A friend of mine who worked in the local sweet shop wanted us to go; I said I would think about it. I would have to save for an outfit and accessories. In the end, I just decided to pass on it; there were way more important things to save for than an outfit I'd maybe wear twice.

But I got lucky; my employers were sending their daughters to the event and wanted me to chaperone them. I didn't really want to; Mandy and Abi were real pains in the ass, but when they said they were paying not only for my ticket but giving me cash for an outfit, I agreed. You don't look a gift horse in the mouth.

The night of the grand opening came, and I was all set to go dancing. I had zero interest in the prince/ duke, whoever it was. I just wanted a night out and to wear my new dress and heels. The giggle twins, Mandy and Abi, took forever to get ready. When they finally appeared, it was like 1985 had thrown up on them. There was no way I was hanging with that fashion nightmare all night.

Once we arrived, I spotted Charlie waiting for us; I was a good friend and had given her a heads-up about the 80's rejects I had to babysit. To give her credit, she didn't die of laugher or roll her eyes. She complimented them, and we all headed for the doors.

The queue was unbelievable, again lucky for us, Mandy and Abi's dad was a big deal in accounting, and we all had VIP tickets. It was as we made our way to the big burly guy guarding the door, that I spotted Precious and Divine. Looking them up and down, I had a new love for the giggle twins and their love for "vintage" club wear. My ex-stepsisters looked like men in really bad drag. I love drag queens; they give the best makeup tips. I just know that if any caught sight of these two, they would be hanging up the sequins and fake lashes for good. It was tragic.

Since I moved out, I had dyed my hair white blonde and got a tan. So, they didn't even recognise me as I walked past in my aqua silk mini dress and "glass" shoes; the woman in the little boutique had told me they were made of lead crystal. They weighed a heck of a lot, but they were so pretty, and I really loved rocking the cinders look. The owner was pleased to sell them; they were a tiny size four, and she had been trying to shift them for months. It seemed that Lady Luck was really paying up.

The club was already packed, and the music was loud. Charlie didn't have VIP access, so she headed for the dance floor to show everyone how dancing should be done, and I went with the girls to the VIP area. That was where the royal dude and his friends and bodyguards would be hanging out. I really hoped for his sake that his royal highness was gay. This was not a safe place for a single guy with a ton of money. Every girl within a hundred-mile radius was trying to get into the club tonight. As the night went on, I was beginning to regret the shoes. Charlie had hooked up with some guy and left, and the giggle twins were more like evil stepsisters now. I needed more of those like I need a hole in the head. They were tired and hot, and they were really pissed that they hadn't even seen the prince/duke/royal dude, whatever. (I found out about an hour later that he was the crown prince of some island in the Mediterranean that I'd never heard of.) I was ready to call it a night.

We handed back our passes, collected our jackets, and headed for the doors. The queue was still huge. I saw Divine and Precious a little way ahead of it. It looked like they hadn't even made it inside. Karma!

We hailed a taxi and got in; we lived on the other side of the city in the fancy part of the suburbs, so we sat back and tried to enjoy the ride. We had only managed to travel three streets when our taxi was hailed to stop. The girls were sleeping, so I asked the driver what was happening. He gave me the "search me" look and hit the brakes.

A man of about thirty appeared at my door; he saw the girls in the back with me and cursed. I just thought he was some weirdo. He then went to the driver's door and wrenched it open.

"In the name of King—something I couldn't pronounce had my life depended on it—I demand you hand over your car." The driver, bless him, tried to explain that he had a fare and there was no way he was handing over his cab to anyone, no matter whose king's name was brought into it.

This didn't appear to go over well with the man who started yelling in a foreign language and waving his arms about like he was trying to take off. In the end, another man approached the car; this one looked way too serious for my liking. He took the driver to the side and slipped him what looked like a grand in cash. Next thing I know, the driver was walking away with the suited dude, and I am sitting in the back of a cab. The child locks are on so I can't get out, and there is a crazy foreign dude climbing into the driver's seat. He didn't even look back at us; he just closed the door and hit the gas.

I wasn't having this. I had signed up to babysit and have a paid night out on the town in a pretty dress and killer heels. Not to be abducted by some loony who didn't seem to get which side of the road he was meant to drive on. I slid the Perspex privacy panel to the side and basically yelled at the guy for a good five minutes. I wanted to know what his problem was and if he wouldn't mind at least letting us out of the car, so we didn't have to be the sideshow to his mental break. Plus, I really needed to get the girls home; their parents would kill me if they weren't home soon.

No reply. Epic. I was stuck with a rude, slightly deranged kidnapper. I needed to call the police; this guy was clearly a danger, and I was not prepared to be a statistic on some crime board. Tonight's freak show was over. I reached for my cell phone and dialled the emergency services.

The second that loony tune heard me say police, the car swerved, and we were heading down a lane I had never noticed in all my time in the city. I then had no idea where the hell we were, and the cell signal was breaking up. I just hoped the fact that I was in a cab and had been on the line for a couple of minutes was long enough for them to trace the call. I really would like to be found before the boys in blue discovered us all chopped up into little pieces and placed in nappy bags along some god-awful B-road in middle England.

The car suddenly stopped, and the criminal in the front seat got out. He paced in front of the stolen car, the head lights glinting off of something on his chest. It looked like medals? I couldn't really tell; it was half hidden by his overcoat. Then it clicked.

Oh man, this couldn't be happening.

If he was who I thought he was, this was way too much. I put all the pieces of recent events together. The accents, the driving, the mention of a king, and now the medals. I was so glad that the girls were still out for the count. I shuddered at the thought of what might have happened if they were awake and aware that they had been essentially kidnapped by the guy they had wanted to meet oh so badly.

He came to the back of the car and opened the door. He looked at the two sleeping sisters beside me and then ordered me out of the car. I got out, figuring I was better able to defend myself and them in the open than in the tiny back seat. He was taller than me by at least a foot and a good hundred pounds heavier. Chocolate brown eyes and thick wavy hair that sat on his collar. He was all brooding and dark. He was quite good looking if you like that sort of thing. He came at me, no warning, no hello, just crazy up in my face.

Hell. No!

I did not sign up for this crap. Dress, shoes, and a paid night off. That is all I agreed to, none of this manhandling by some over-entitled idiot in a dark lane at three in the bloody morning. I dodged him and moved away from the car; I needed to draw him away from the girls. He tried again, and this time I cracked him a good one across his face. My hand hurt like hell, but there was no way he was getting closer.

He seemed to think differently; he tried again. Only this time I stumbled and fell back. The thick mud on the lane clung to my coat and legs, oh and hair. Damn, my shoes; they were covered in thick mud. That was a step too far. Never, and I mean never, mess with a girl's shoes. He offered me his hand, which was weird as he was trying to attack me a second ago. I took it, and once back on my feet, I looked at him. There was something familiar about him; I just couldn't place him.

"You are Ella, yes?"

I nodded but kept myself out of reach. I didn't know this guy, and I really didn't like him knowing my name. He was still a raving loony.

"Who wants to know?"

" I am Prince Xander."

He even did a bow. I rolled my eyes; this still didn't explain the abduction and the attack—oh and the fact that he was a loony.

"Good for you, dude, but I have a question. What the freaking hell are you doing?"

I was so angry and cold, and, well damn, my shoes looked terrible. He was trying to explain, when Mandy woke up and was suddenly all over the guy. They fell to the ground, and her excited screaming woke Abi. I face palmed. This was just getting worse. I was so quitting my job in the morning.

They were like animals, tearing at his clothes and clawing his skin. When Mandy produced a knife and Abi a small jar, things suddenly took a nasty turn. I tried to get them to talk to me, but they were having none of it. They wanted a piece of him to keep.

Because that's not at all creepy!

He was pinned; the knife was getting closer to his chest, and there was no way I was going to let them mutilate him. Sure, he had pulled some dick moves tonight, but to be filleted for it seemed a bit much. I tried to pull Abi off, but Mandy whipped around and sliced my leg with the knife.

Now I was really mad.

They were out of control, and I had no doubt they were willing to kill the guy just for some hair or a few drops of blood. I swear I will never understand teenage girls, and I was one!

I took off my left shoe and held it by the front with the heel exposed. I only intended to get her to drop the knife. However, Mandy turned and saw me poised and ready to disarm her, and she came at me. In that moment it was her or me, and frankly, I like me more. I hit her hard. The weight of the shoe caught the bridge of her nose; I heard the crack of splintering bone, but she still kept coming. I slipped in the mud, and suddenly she was on me, and my shoe was between us. I felt her blade puncture the flesh of my shoulder. I cried out in pain and gathered all my strength to free my arms and get her off me.

Everything became very still then; Mandy was no longer a wild cat on top of me. I blinked away the tears so I could see what was happening, maybe the cops had shown up at last?

What I saw I will never forget. In my desperation to free myself, I had forgotten about the shoe. The heel of my glass slipper was imbedded in her right eye socket. All the way to the hilt. Mandy was dead. Forever frozen in that shocked moment when her world ended.

IT WASN'T long after that, that the police finally showed up. The prince explained the whole thing, and I was taken away for questioning. Abi was found to have high levels of cocaine in her system, and I was pretty sure that Mandy's autopsy report would show the same thing. I felt guilty then, how had they got a hold of the drugs? I guess I'll never know. I am totally fired, probably with a restring order too.

I was finally released, after a lot of questioning, and no charges were ever brought against me as it was deemed to be self-defence. Outside the station I was greeted by Xander.

"Before you open your mouth, I need a shower, clean clothes, a coffee, and my shoe back."

Xander held up an evidence bag containing my shoe. "They no longer need it; it's been tested."

I take the bag and heave at the sight of the mud, blood, and brain matter still attached to my beautiful shoe. I was not going to enjoy cleaning that up.

"Great, now first things first, I have to clean Mandy off my shoe."

Holding the bag at arm's length, I look at Xander who is just smiling and totally calm. Maybe accidental death by shoe is normal where he comes from.

"You know, I didn't even want to meet you, I only went because I got a free night out and a great pair of shoes."

THE CURSE

BASED ON RAPUNZELL

There was no way around the truth; everyone was bound to find out. Which is why they had to hide her. Nothing hurts more than losing a child; the pain is beyond measure, far beyond the reaches of the darkest imagination. A mother that loves her child is a powerful thing, a natural thing. But what does that mother do when her beautiful child is possessed?

The day Martha came to take their baby girl away was the worst day. The day Amanda swallowed the bittersweet pill of loss and relief. The loss of her only daughter, the only child she would ever bear, and yet it sickened her for more than just the physical loss. Her burden had been lifted, an issue removed, and trouble gone. She hated herself for these thoughts and feelings. She loved her child more than life itself, but she knew she could never have her back. No matter the love she had for her beautiful baby; the child had to go.

Martha knew what she was getting into; being a witch, she was used to aiding those who needed her gifts. This case, however, was the most extreme she had ever been asked to assist with. The church had told the child's parents to pray for the girl's deliverance, to anoint her with oil and say blessings over her. The local priest attended the home of the family on a regular basis; even with the divine on his side the baby girl still remained "possessed."

Martha knew the child was different. She had a pure soul, but it was the other part of her that seemed to cause all the issues. As a child, Rachael, was a delight; she grew into a beautiful and adventurous child with the most gorgeous blonde hair. It resembled spun gold and platinum. The otherness that hung about her wasn't fully revealed to the witch until the child was five years old.

Martha and Rachael lived on a farm a mile from anyone, and the wards that the witch had erected meant that the ramblers or random visitors would never find the house. They just arrived on the other side of the property boundary, none the wiser for the magical detour. Which was just as well, because what Martha witnessed a week after the child's fifth birthday shocked her.

Rachael was playing in the garden; she was a loving child and of late, had shown a real interest in the wildlife that lived in the thicket of trees just to the left of their home. Martha always wondered why the animals stayed away from the little girl. She was quiet and slow in her movements, always used her most gentle voice and yet, the animals would flee from her. It broke Martha's heart to watch her child—as that was how she saw her—cry into her perfect tiny hands at the lack of the contact she so craved with the creatures who shared the land with her.

The day that changed everything will stay with the witch forever. It explained so much, but tore a ragged hole in their perfect family life. It became no longer just about hiding her away from those who may see a resemblance to her birth parents. Now it was about the darkness inside her.

For that was the secret within the secret. Martha had tried to glamour the girl so she could be closer to her mother and make friends. It just wasn't possible, the spell just wouldn't stick.

It was a sunny morning, and a fawn had entered the garden where Rachael had been playing with her animals. She loved her toy animals the best, as they never ran from her when she wanted to touch them and study their little glass eyes. On that morning however, the true nature of her otherness was revealed. That tea party with her stuffed animals in the sunshine changed their lives forever.

Rachael's beautiful mane of golden tresses had always grown very fast and very thick. That day it was tied in a simple ponytail that rested along her little spine, the very tips brushing the clover beneath her. The golden strands were catching the sun, and her head seemed to glow with radiant light. The fawn came closer to the child; maybe it was the smell of the berries Racheal had put in her little sugar bowl for the tea, that had attracted the creature. Sugar was bad for your teeth she had told Martha when she had offered some lumps of it from the pantry.

"Fruit is better, and my animals really like berries."

For whatever reason, that day the fawn was brave enough to come into the garden and approach Rachael. It was a moment before she noticed her new companion. Martha made a dash for the camera to capture this first for her daughter; back at the window, she raised the camera to her eye to focus the frame and then froze. Rachael had her hand raised towards the deer with her tiny palm filled with berries; her silent plea was clear—"please be my friend."

As the young deer took a few slow steps closer and stretched its graceful neck to sample the sweet treat held out to it, everything changed. The camera shutter went off as Rachael's beautiful hair whipped up suddenly, as if caught in a strong gust of wind. It dragged the small girl about; she was a puppet, caught in an invisible hand that pulled the child round as if she weighed nothing at all.

Rachael was too shocked to cry out at first, but then she found her voice. The scream bubbled up from a deep place inside her, the place where the worst nightmares live. Just as the first strains of her high-pitched squeal escaped her lips, Martha had unfrozen, dropped the camera, and ran for the back door to save her child from an unknown danger.

Rachael's long golden hair was no longer a beautiful waterfall of shining gold, it was a weapon, a hangman's rope. It was deadly. The thick tail of hair coiled itself around the fawn's neck. Rachael's screams were hysterical; it was a sound that could chill one's blood.

Almost to her child now, Martha watched as little Rachael thrashed and screamed as if controlled by an unseen force. She was thrown backward towards her forgotten tea party which had not so long ago given her such joy. It was then that the scene took a rapid turn. It all happened so fast. Martha reached her child just as her hair whipped viciously back and then gently fell against Rachael's quivering back. But it was the loud crack of the fawn's neck that froze them; that would never be forgotten. Martha hid the little girl's face in her chest. She watched in horror as the creature, an innocent child, much like her own, collapsed into the clover beneath its hooves. Its huge brown eyes were glassy, devoid of life. Martha knew that this had not been Rachael's doing. The tiny body she held was shaking; she was terrified.

There was something within her though; it was evil, there was no doubt about that. The only comfort to be had in that moment was that it only seemed to be strong enough to control her hair. Martha prayed that it would never gain any more strength.

Why had her hair not attacked me?

Then she remembered she always wore a protection spell, ever since the feeling of otherness had hung about the child. The question then was what the hell was she going to do to protect Rachael essentially from herself?

TWELVE YEARS LATER . . .

Racheal had learned to live with her affliction as best as she could. Martha was a powerful magic user and had cast many charms and wards so that Rachael's hair no longer attacked anyone that came too close, including animals. In the end though, at around the age of thirteen, Martha stopped taking Rachael out into the wider world. By the time she was seventeen, Rachael was lonely and resentful of her virtual prisoner status.

Imagine being seventeen and never having friends; imagine the complete feeling of loneliness. Apart from her mother who was a constant companion, she was utterly alone. Rachael hated her life, and like every other girl her age, she was desperate for friends and her first love. Over time, she argued with Martha about the reasons why she would be fine in the outside world, how the magic would hold, and there really wasn't a need to worry; there hadn't been an incident for years. The answer was always no, and they fought for days, both becoming resentful of their circumstances. The more Martha tried to explain, the more Rachael's temper would increase.

It reached the breaking point two months after her seventeenth birthday; she became so agitated that somehow, she managed to break through the binding spell. Thankfully, Martha had preempted this and managed to repair the damage and cast a stronger binding spell over Rachael's hair while it was already reaching for her throat. After that, there was no more talk about going outside for a while. However, it was becoming clear to Martha that Rachael was turning into quite a volatile young woman, and therefore, extra care needed to be taken. Rachael was becoming extremely dangerous.

It was with a heavy heart that she decided it was best that Rachael be kept in isolation, shrouded by magic, where she could live out her days safely. It was a hard decision to make and one Martha did not relish. She treated Rachael as if she were her own child; she loved her like only a mother could. She had tried everything to remedy this curse that lived within the child; nothing worked.

Martha recalled the day she had tried to cut Rachael's hair. She still bore the scars from the cutting shears that had ended up dug deep into her flesh; she walked with a limp now thanks to that fateful day.

Getting Rachael to the abandoned folly by the river was no easy feat. The home was beautiful; Martha had seen to that. It contained a library, music room, kitchen, bedroom, and a tower to take in the views. It was of the finest stone and, thanks to a few spells, would never age or fall into disrepair. Rachael was in love with the house; she ran through the rooms excitedly choosing where her favourite objects and keepsakes would live, and tried to decide which room she would use as a bedroom, the actual bedroom or the tower. It was when Martha came to leave that she realised that she was going to be living in this house alone. It was a prison. The rage overcame her once more.

Martha made it out of the house before the enchantment surrounding Rachael's hair broke again. She stood outside the small folly a moment to catch her breath, and then began to throw up the magical wards and concealing the doors and windows. Rachael would still be able to see out, but no one would be able to see in; to the casual observer this folly would appear abandoned and dilapidated. Deeply hurt by what she had had to do, Martha left the riverbank and her child; the sound of breaking furniture followed her as she made her way back through the forest.

Rachael had never been so angry; she was a prisoner in a gilded cage. The food magically replenished itself whenever she ate something. There was always fresh water, and her home never became dirty even though she made no attempts to clean.

All that time alone had a rather damaging effect on Rachael, her mind imploded. Humans are a social species; they thrive on that essential contact with their own kind. Rachael needed to feel valued and loved and alive. She needed to be a part of the world to truly live. But she wasn't, she wasn't a part of any world, and gradually, piece by shattered piece, her mind unraveled.

Time meant little when one is a prisoner in solitary confinement, so she wasn't sure whether a day, a month, a year, a decade, or longer had passed. There were no mirrors within her house. She had no idea how aged she had become. The one thing she was sure of was her hair, her beautiful cursed hair. It swept the floor and fell around her feet in pools of gold. It was unchanged. Forever vibrant and strong.

The day she saw a stranger approach her secluded home was a great cause for concern. She knew two things must have happened. The wards hiding the folly from the world must be gone. This also meant that her mother, Martha, was dead. The heartbreak she felt was all consuming. The guilt was overwhelming, and her rage was overpowering. The anger crashed over her in waves that felt like they would tear her apart.

How long has she been here?

How long had it been since she had seen her mother's face?

How lonely and broken had she truly become?

Looking at the door, she realised a horrible truth. Now she that had the freedom she had craved for so long, she didn't want it.

She watched the woman approach and laugh, so even after all these years alone there was no prince to save her like in the story books she had read when she was a child. No, it was just some woman walking through the woods, a woman who had stumbled into a clearing containing a beautiful home with a deadly secret.

Rachael watched the woman approach with envious eyes; it wasn't fair. She watched the sun glint off of chestnut brown hair, and the rosy cheeks that spoke of days spent in the sun. The anger within her boiled over. How dare this woman come here and mock her with her freedom and happiness when all Rachael had was this house and her anger and her hair.

In a moment of absolute fury, she decided that this woman, this stranger didn't deserve the happiness; she did. Let this stranger be locked away in this prison; let her go slowly mad within the gilded cage. It was her turn to be free. She had waited long enough, and now there was no one, no magic, and no reason, for her to stay within these walls a moment longer.

Unfortunately, Rachael had forgotten the consequences of being around others. There was no way that she could just simply grab the woman, put her in the house, lock the door, and walk away. There were other things to consider, like her cursed hair.

It was too late by the time her mind cooled enough to realise her error. Meters of her golden hair flew about her the second the door was opened. Unlike when she was a child, her hair was much longer, and so the thrashing of it didn't affect her as it had back then. It cascaded around her like a golden sea. The other woman had turned at the sound of the door opening, only to be greeted by Rachael's hair wrapping her from ankles to neck. Rachael stared in a mixture of horror and manic glee.

It was over quickly, as it had been with the deer all those years ago. Only this time, Rachael felt real fear and real guilt for what had happened. If she had only stayed in the house and heeded her mother's warning; then here wouldn't be a mummified woman trapped within her hair. Her loneliness was a small price to pay when compared to murder.

With tears in her eyes, she yanked on her hair and watched it unfurl from the now dead woman. It returned to its usual innate self. Mouthing the word "sorry" to her victim, Rachael gathered up her hair, backed into her home, and closed the door. Still clutching her tresses to her chest, she headed to the kitchen. There was no way she was willing to live like this; there was no way she could allow that to happen again. Reaching blindly into one of the drawers, she pulled out a pair of cutting shears. The second they were in her hand, the hair, her hair, the crowning glory that caused so much suffering, attacked.

MANY YEARS LATER . . .

The folly was found again, this time by an architect. The land had been bought by a wealthy business owner who wanted to use the property for a holiday home. When the man tried to enter the house, he found the door jammed shut. Looking through the windows, he was shocked to see the remains of what appeared to be two desiccated females; one was on the kitchen table surrounded by long dead flowers, and the other was in the middle of the kitchen floor with a pair of cutting shears near her right hand. The only thing that was very out of place—other than the dead bodies in the middle of the kitchen—was that most of the room was covered in masses of golden hair.

As his hand touched the window, something shot out of the gloomy corner of the room and thumped against the window, rattling the panes. Stepping back in shock, he looked to see what had caused the bang. All the colour drained from his face as he realised the thing that was rapping on the window was a lock of the golden hair.

TINY VIRUS

BASED ON THUMBELINA

Germs, disgusting microscopic, destructive entities. They will wipe out the human race someday; in the distant future, there will be a virus so devastating that we will not be able to contain it or cure it with our surgeries and chemicals. So, let's take a moment to think about that possible future. A future where a tiny vial that contains a lethal pathogen code-named THUMBELINA exists.

Why would we suspend reality, you're thinking, and create this terrible world-altering virus? What if at this moment, in a lab somewhere, a clever scientist has already created such a thing.

What if this isn't hypothetical at all?

Somewhere in the world right now, there is a secret facility that cultivates highly advanced genetically modified foodstuffs and animals. Now imagine that somehow, some of the GM corn accidentally became contaminated with a form of weaponised bubonic plague. Sounds far- fetched right? But mistakes happen every day in labs all over the world. So, it's really not unimaginable, is it?

World leaders could, and possibly already, cover up major accidents that take place in facilities that we, the public, know nothing about.

The agent code-named THUMBELINA came into being by the cross contamination of two highly developed, yet extremely different, entities. Unfortunately, this accident was missed, and the corn was sent for its usual batch of routine tests.

One of the tests is to feed the milled corn to animals, to ensure it is safe for human consumption. Animals in themselves are a wild card. Why, you ask? Because they carry hitchhikers also known as fleas. The fleas became carries for the virus and spread it from animal to animal in a very short space of time. THUMBELINA was now in active population.

Within the space of two weeks, twenty percent of the entire facility was locked down, quarantined, and for all intents and purposes, forgotten about by the government that set it up in the first place. THUMBELINA mutated quickly and was now the world's most deadly contagion that had ever been recorded.

Professor Jarvis was the leader in the field of biochemical warfare. When she heard of the new highly contagious virus she was horrified and spent many hours studying the infected as best as she could. She noticed that depending on the host, the symptoms and rapidity of the illness progression differed greatly.

For example, the first host, who we shall name Patient Zero, was a mouse; now, the mice had been fed a mixture of seed and milled GM corn for precisely five months and sixteen days. It took Patient Zero three days to reach what Prof. Jarvis hypothesised was the last stages of the infection's life cycle. Once the rodents had died, more tests were undertaken. It was discovered that their organs had liquefied after death, or right before, leaving what appeared to be a skin sack sitting in a puddle of foul-smelling bodily fluids.

It was also noted by Prof. Jarvis, that each rodent that she examined was completely devoid of fleas, bone marrow, and all soft tissues. As the virus spread from species to species, she watched in fascination. Depending on the next host's diet and breed, the presentation of the virus changed the symptomatic output of the patient. To her horror, it was also mutating at an alarming rate. This new and disturbing finding caused her to take on the incredibly dangerous task of collecting samples from each species that has contracted THUMBELINA. Thus, beginning a lengthy process of trying to create either an antiviral or a cure. At the very least, an antiviral would slow down the progression. Hopefully.

Things seem to be advancing as well as could be expected, until it spread to the amphibians. Once the toads became infected, the entire game changed. The toads were living in biologically altered habitats. The origins of the introduction of THUMBELINA was unknown to the professor; she could only assume that somehow the water supply had become infected. This posed new challenges, for her and the two biologists she had managed to recruit, on this mission to contain the virus and potentially save mankind.

Toads by nature are quite hardy. However, when startled or threatened, they have a nasty habit of squirting a toxin at their would-be attacker. This is called the bufotoxin. When the toads came into contact with the virus, their bufotoxin levels altered immeasurably. Now, the toads were constantly secreting this altered toxin rather than just as a form of defence. The knock-on effect of this new mutation of THUMBELINA meant that every aquatic animal and vegetation that came into contact with either the host or the water supply became infected with a brand new strain.

Prof. Jarvis watched in horror as entire biodomes of amphibians, fish, and vegetation died within a week, sometimes in as little as a few hours. It was then that she reached the conclusion; THUMBELINA was never going to be curable.

The facility had been on lockdown since Patient Zero had been identified and then subsequently died. This, however, didn't seem to bother the pioneering microbiologist, Prof. Nugent. He had, against the advice of every authority who knew about the facility, decided to return to the site after its closing.

When Prof. Nugent arrived and practically beat the front door down, Jarvis felt she had no choice but to allow him entry. If there was one thing that had been drummed into her by the officials who came to evacuate staff, it was that no matter what happened, no one must ever know this place or these experiments existed.

As soon as the new professor gained access, he examined the timeline of THUMBELINA and its mutations. He was lost for words; the rapid spread of the virus was unprecedented. It was highly adaptable and resistant to all strains of antidote that had been created thus far. He asked Prof. Jarvis and her team for every piece of evidence, every scrap of data and any physical samples they had collected since the outbreak.

Together, the team of four worked tirelessly in their tiny section of the facility, trying to find a way to at least slow THUMBELINA down. It was during a routine check of the aviary that one of the biologists suffered a tear in their biohazard suit. This on its own would not have posed a great risk, however, he didn't notice the breach and then continued his tour and entered the amphibians' biodome. As soon as his hand was submerged in the water to collect the latest sample, his fate was sealed. The bufotoxin that the toads secrete causes skin irritation in human, usually completely harmless. In this case, it was weaponised, and as soon as Mike scratched absently as his irritated skin, he created microscopic tears with his fingernails which allowed THUMBELINA into his bloodstream. Mike became patient zero of the human race. For any biologist, the jump from domestic or wild animals to the human population is their worse night- mare; they all hope it will never come to pass.

By the time Mike contracted THUMBELINA and it mixed with his own DNA, the mutations the virus had already undertaken when combined with the bufotoxin were so extreme that Mike's body treated this new unity like a cancer. It sat in his body multiply- ing, convincing healthy cells it was meant to be there.

The other horrific outcome to this new and tragic development was that THUMBELINA was now airborne. Tests on Mike's blood revealed that he was growing tumors at an alarming rate in all areas of his body, but especially around his vital organs. It also became clear that human to human infection was through microfluid contamination. At the time of his exposure, Mike also had a harmless strain of the common cold. He had been too embarrassed to tell the team of his mishap in both the aviary and the amphibian biodomes, and he became symptomatic, unintentionally spreading this new strain of THUMBELINA to his colleague Matilda.

As soon as the professors realised that there was a real chance they could all be infected, they set about the grim task of killing every creature and all vegetation within the biodomes and the storage centres. It was to them a great failure to know that they would never survive this outbreak. To have witnessed such an aggressive, highly contagious, and extremely adaptable virus such as this. It completely crippled their facility in a matter of weeks; it was truly on an apocalyptic scale.

The only silver lining, if you can call it that, was that each habitat and lab was fitted with the latest and very efficient doomsday kit. This kit was effectively napalm in a vacuum. Once the kill codes were entered into the computer, each area would be instantly incinerated to the point of dust. It was Prof. Jarvis' hope, a relatively quick and painless death. She knew that once the codes were set it had a domino effect, and there would be no escape for her or her colleagues.

They spent forty-eight hours observing Mike and Matilda before calling it. Within that time, Prof. Nugent made an unimaginable discovery. Unbeknownst to Prof.-Jarvis, Nugent, had given both Mike and Matilda another weaponised idea. Namely influenza. The results varied greatly between the patients. Mike began to secret albumin from his pores, and huge blisters began to appear on his extremities. He had a mutated version of bullous pemphigoid, an autoimmune skin disease. He was also dehydrating rapidly. However, Matilda, by some miracle, seemed to be stabilizing; the tumors, though wide-spread, were not as aggressive or as large as Mike's. This could have been for several reasons, but the outlook was encouraging. Her DNA had caused THUMBELINA to mutate again, and with the introduction of the flu virus, it seemed to have caused THUMBELINA to enter a form of stasis. This gave the professors hope, and they decided to extend their observation period of both patients to see if anything changed.

Within fourteen hours, Mike was dead. He had suffered catastrophic dehydration and loss of vital proteins. His heart had failed. Matilda, on the other hand, was still stable and Prof. Nugent had decided to try and synthesise an antiviral from her blood. Their first few attempts were unsuccessful. THUMBELINA was hardy and very much wanting to continue inhabiting the host. They had extended their window by seven days, and there was still no sign of an antiviral.

Prof. Jarvis was losing all hope and decided that is was time to end this for all their sakes. Hope was only useful for so long, and they were running out of water and food. Soon they wouldn't have to worry about THUMBELINA; it would be the slow painful death of dehydration and starvation.

She headed for the mainframe computer to enter the kill codes and end this failed attempt to control this outbreak and find the cure. It was then that Prof. Nugent came running through to find her. He was elated; Matilda's tumors were shrinking! She was fighting the virus without medical intervention. He had already taken more blood and was sure, this time, he could make a rudimentary vaccine so they could all leave this facility.

It took a moment for it to sink in, they could leave? She couldn't believe it. Prof. Nugent asked for forty-eight hours to get something together. It wasn't standard to work so fast; in fact it was miles too short a window, however, this was a do or die situation.

TWO DAYS LATER . . .

The three biologists left the facility and put it on

lockdown. They had survived THUMBELINA, and now they carried the possible cure for the illness, should it ever break out.

Exactly six weeks and five days after leaving the hell that THUMBELINA had wreaked over their lives, Prof. Nugent and Prof. Jarvis were struck down by an unknown virus. The symptoms were similar to Ebola but highly accelerated. Both were taken to their local hospitals and treatment in quarantine began. Matilda recovered, and thankfully there were no lasting signs of her encounter with THUMBELINA.

Two weeks after the professors were admitted to different hospitals, both were moved to a special unit in the south of England. Sadly, they died within hours of arriving. Due to the nature of their illness and subsequent deaths, they had left a trail of blood, body secretions, hair, and DNA across three counties. The vaccine that they had taken to prevent THUMBELINA had not worked, and unbeknown to them, they had both contracted the virus. The vaccine had caused THUMBELINA to mutate further. It was now active within highly populated areas. The end of the modern word as we know it had finally arrived.

The most disturbing part? A government scientist who knew where the professors had been working had managed to obtain a vial of Prof. Nugent's blood and a vial of the contagion, THUMBELINA. The most dangerous super virus was now in the hands of one of the superpowers of Earth.

This is all conjecture, however, what if this actually happened? Something as tiny as THUMBELINA, a microscopic organism, could wipe us off the planet in a matter of months.

TROUGH

BASED ON THE THREE LITTLE PIGS

Hannah Frankle had been obsessed with pigs all her life. It was a deep-rooted love that had grown from living on her grandmother's farm as a child. Granny Bess had always kept a sow, and once a year a neighbour's boar was brought in for mating. There were always new piglets the following year, and Hannah loved them all. She taught them tricks and fed them treats. In one of the last litters, Granny Bess's sow had produced a runt. Hannah fell hopelessly in love with the tiny piglet; it was constantly bullied by its bigger siblings and had to fight for his share of the mother's milk and later for his place at the trough. Hannah called the tiny pig Rodney, and for that whole summer they were inseparable.

Rodney only grew to double his birth weight, but his hearty appetite for life matched the one he had for food. It was this that gave Hannah a sense of comfort; she knew full well that the bigger hogs were going to the slaughter, and that thought made her sick. But that is what happens on a farm, and Granny Bess was not one to suffer the tears of a child over an animal.

"When I die, you can do with the farm as you want, Hannah. But until that day, the pigs make money, and they are going to slaughter."

Hannah nodded, hating her Grandmother in that moment. She held Rodney close, knowing that he would never go to slaughter. No one would pay for a runty little scrap of nothing.

Granny Bess lived a long life and loved her farm. She taught Hannah all she could and left more and more of the management to her as she grew. It was fifteen years after that day beside the trough discussing the fate of the hogs, that Granny Bess died. Being a strong country woman, she hadn't died in her bed; she was out at the age of eighty-nine, milking her cows by hand as she always had. She was found about an hour or so after death, her grey head leaning against the cow she had been milking.

Hannah had been devastated. She had loved her Grandmother; there was no other family for her now, and she realised that she was alone in the world. Even Rodney was getting old in years. She hoped he would not leave her yet; she needed her little pig more than ever.

In the year that followed, Hannah made the farm into a sanctuary; not a single animal was killed for food, and over time they all lost their fear and relaxed when they realised that the slaughter house truck was never returning to the farm. Hannah and Rodney, who by then was twenty years old, loved their life on the land and thought nothing would ever steal their happiness.

Life, as everyone knows, has a beginning and an end; at twenty-two and a half, Rodney died in his sleep. Hannah mourned him deeply. She had loved him almost her whole life, and now he wasn't going to be there to greet her every morning with his pink tail wagging, making his adorable squeal of delight. Rodney knew that when Hannah was awake that the day's adventure could begin, and Hannah loved how happy he was to just be alive.

ONE OF THE old farm hands had spotted poachers along the tree line of the far field. They had wolfhounds with them. He was concerned for the livestock, especially the pigs as they had just welcomed new piglets the day before.

He was right to worry; three nights later, Hannah was woken by the most terrible screaming. The poachers had sent their hounds onto her land, and they had let them into her pig pen. Hannah had only a few pigs, and the sound of their screaming ripped her from sleep and out into the night, rifle in hand.

The poachers were still there, along with two wolfhounds that were ripping her piglets apart. One of the poachers was busy gutting one of the older pigs. Hannah had intended to fire warning shots, but after the sight of her pigs being mauled and gutted on her land . . . she fired.

The poacher with the knife went down, blood trickling from his now smashed eye socket. The other had ran when hearing the shots; she aimed and fired again, taking out his left knee. His scream drowned out the sound of her dying pets, but her rage had not yet been calmed. She didn't kill the hounds; they had been trained to kill by the scum, now dead or dying.

As soon as she had scared the dogs off, she went to check on her pigs. She saw the sow was badly hurt, and three of her piglets were dead. She looked everywhere for the three unaccounted piglets; she couldn't look at the body of her other piglet yet, the one that was half butchered with its snout cut off and its throat slit. After searching fruitlessly for over an hour in the dark, she had to admit she was never going to find them. Hannah needed to focus on her sow; she was losing blood fast. She needed a vet.

The two poachers were another matter; Hannah was not one for killing, but she had the right to shoot anyone on her land, and she needed to protect what was hers. David, her farm hand, was all for calling the police, which is what they should have done. But in the end, it was decided that the dead man would be fed to the remaining pigs, and the other who was unable to walk due to a shattered kneecap, would have his tongue cut out and dumped in the trees at the back of the far field beyond her fences. That was where the wild boar lived, and she was sure they would take care of the rest of him.

It was a full month before the wolfhounds were back; this time there were four of them, and the poachers were armed. Word was out that two of their community were missing, and the last farm they had planned to rob was the Frankle estate.

Hannah had been afraid this would happen. She had just finished dissolving the bones of the last poachers in hydrochloric acid; the wild boars and her pigs had picked the bodies clean in little over three days. But now she was faced with more than before, and these guys had rifles as well as hunting knives. David and Jerry, his apprentice, had taken up posts in the barn loft and the disused dairy. They were armed and ready to take down anyone who got within range.

Hannah could feel the tension building in her; she would not lose more animals. Gertie, her sow, had survived the last attack— just barely. There was no way she could be put through that again. As the hounds got closer, the pigs began to squeal. Hannah was watching from the upstairs window, rifle loaded at her side. The window was open, but she couldn't be seen; the night was ink black, and the windows were ebony against the it. As long as they didn't shine their torches up at the windows, she would be safe—until she started firing.

David had bought them all night vision goggles; seemed extreme to her, but as she slipped them on and could see the men approaching from the direction of the far field, she was grateful he had thought of them.

The pigs' squealing crescendoed as the hounds reached the sty, and the poachers approached on the wet grass behind them. Hannah raised her rifle and took aim. The killing was over quickly; Hannah took down two of the four, and Jerry and David cleaned up the other two. This time, one of the hounds was shot; it had broken into the sty, and David made the call. Hannah was upset by its death but understood that it was to save her pigs.

THE NEXT MORNING, the bodies were hidden, and the hound was skinned; its pelt was hung on the spot where the poachers entered. On his return, David splayed a little body on the lawn. Hannah watched from the kitchen window. She was sharpening her butcher knives in readiness. She intended to dismember the poachers and store them in her chest freezer, then bring them out when the pigs had finished the first lot. Putting down her weapon of choice, she left the kitchen and went to stand with David over the small form. She already knew what it would be.

"I found her up by the fence line, right where the poachers break in."

"It's okay. I knew this was likely." "Want me to bury her with the others?"

"Yes, please, I just hope this is the last one we ever

find."

TWO YEARS LATER . . .

Hannah woke up on a crisp February morning to a blood bath. All her pigs, apart from Gertie who was once again badly hurt, were dead. This time there had been no hounds to warn the pigs. They had all been shot in the head. They must have used a silencer because she hadn't heard a thing all night. As if it wasn't enough to just kill them, they had then broken in and cut the animals to ribbons. It was all just for sport.

More bodies were buried, and Hannah was ready to give up and move on. So much death, both by her own hand and by the poachers and hounds. This was not how she imagined it would be.

~

DEEP in the woods beyond the boundary line, another family was beginning to make its way to the fence of the far field. Pigs are clever animals, and these three pigs were on their way home.

The original piglets that had escaped by some miracle the night of the first break in, when the hounds had killed so many of their siblings, had fled from the farm and headed into the woods. They had managed to remain hidden, and eventually, mated with some wild boar that had been roaming the area. The three pigs that headed back to the farm were the descendants of the union. Their curved tusks and muscular bodies made them hardier than their domesticated parents. With the rough coats and swiftness that comes naturally to wild boar, these little pigs were hard to see and even harder to catch.

They knew the dangers of the woods, the hounds that roamed with poachers and the owls who would carry off a newborn hog if given the chance. However, these boars were different; they felt a deep yearning to be close to the farm. So, on a cold spring morning, six years after their parents fled the farm, they headed home.

"Hannah, bloody hell, you won't believe what I have just seen in the far field!"

Hannah watched as Jerry dashed about the office, looking for his key to the ammo safe. Her blood ran cold, not more hounds or dead pigs. It had been relentless the last six years; she couldn't take anymore.

"If it's more dead animals then I am done. I will sell up; I can't take any more of this."

"It's animals all right, but they aren't dead—yet."

"What the hell do you mean yet? Are they in pain?"

Hannah was out of her chair and heading for the jeep outside. Jumping in, she gunned the engine, and before Jerry could stop her, headed for the far field.

What she saw was three beautiful boars. There was something a little off about them; their ears were overly large, and they were a wee bit too pinkish about the snout, but they were adorable. There was no way she was going to let Jerry kill them or call animal control. These creatures were killed just for being what they were, and she would be no party to that. There was enough blood on her hands.

The three animals observed her as she looked down at them. They didn't charge when she jumped from the jeep. They didn't move at all. They simply stood and watched her with their dark intelligent eyes. After a while, the biggest of the three took a few steps towards Hannah, pawed at the soft earth, and then with a final look, turned and headed back into the forest. Its companions followed close behind.

"What in heavens name was that all about?" Jerry had arrived but had hung back to watch. He had his gun but had a feeling that had he taken a shot he would be the next one fed to the pigs down the hill.

"I think it's time I got some more piglets, Jerry." Hannah was good as her word; three tiny piglets came and joined her on the farm. They were perfectly pink and happy. Hannah felt the hole that had been left in her heart since the loss of her last sounder begin to mend. This time she felt these little, perfect piglets would live to see old age.

A week and a half after their arrival, the boars came back to visit the new additions to the farm. Jerry, of course, overreacted.

"The heck are you doing letting them near the babies; they will eat them!"

Hannah just shook her head and left them be, they were, after all, distant cousins, and she was sure no harm would come to them. It had taken her a while to work out that these boars were the descendants of her lost three little pigs. It was touching that they had come back to the farm, and there was no way she was going to discourage them. She truly believed no harm would befall them in regard to the boars.

That night when she visited her new additions before turning in, she noticed the boars were still milling about the fence. This was curious behaviour; they were not in any way domesticated, and boars by nature tend to keep as far from humans as they could get. So, to find the three of them rooting through the grass made her wonder what was going on.

"Well, my little boars, I don't know why you are here, but you are very welcome. If you are still here in the morning, I'll get you a nice chunk of poacher from the freezer." She thought for a moment. "I'll have Jerry drag the old trough out for you too. Goodnight."

She had a peek into the new Wendy house she had built for her piglets; it was made of bricks, and she had given it a wooden roof and filled it with straw to keep them dry and warm. It was the most extravagant sty in all of England.

Squealing ripped her from sleep. At first, she thought it was a nightmare; she had the same one over and over again. It had been months since the last poacher had come to take a look and ended up in the freezer for his trouble. She waited in the dark, her breathing ragged and her heart beating in her ears. If she was to save her new piglets, she needed to calm down. The squealing came again, and she just knew the poachers were back. Leaping from the bed, she pulled on her boots and grabbed her rifle. Enough was enough.

The sky was clear; the moon was a milky disc in the inky blue night. It gave ample light to see by. As Hannah raced around the house and down the path to the sty, she prayed for her pigs; they needed to be okay.

What she saw was beyond her imagination. The boars were still there, and they were protecting her piglets from what looked like an actual wolf! This one was alone, and its blood was up. She knew poachers had sent it in here; there were no wolves in the area. In fact, there were no wild wolves in England at all. As the wind blew gently in her direction, she caught the scent of fresh blood. Hannah kept her rifle up and searched the ground; she soon found the slumped form of a poacher. He had been gored; his entrails were steaming in the cold night. Now she understood. The boars had been waiting. Somehow they had known this was going to happen and had stayed to protect their kin. She needed to help them.

A squeal broke the silence, and Hannah raised her rifle. The wolf had attacked the smaller of the three boars; his yellow teeth had snapped the bones of its back leg. For the first time in her life, Hannah set her sights on an animal. This was not going to happen again. Not on her farm.

She was about to pull the trigger as the beast moved in for the killing blow. The injured boar was helpless. Hannah was ready to fire and end the wolf's life, then the situation changed. She watched as the wolf was thrown from its feet. The two uninjured boars had charged it. The whimper that the wolf made told her that it was fatally wounded. One of the boars rammed the prone wolf in its under belly again and again. Until the whimpering stopped, and the boar's face was a bloody mess of flesh and fur.

Then everything went quiet.

Hannah woke in the sty the next morning; she had taken the boar with the broken leg in with her piglets. Its leg was a mess, but she had set it and hoped after a few weeks rest it would be strong enough to return home to the forest. The other two had chosen to remain out in the open. Ever vigilant. Pulling hay from her hair, Hannah looked around her in the early dawn light. Her three little pigs and her boar were a pile of pink and brown in the yellow straw.

"You are the bravest little pigs I have ever known."

SHE TOUCHED the little boar on the back and felt it stretch a little. "And you are the bravest boar in the whole world."

The boars never left the farm, but they didn't stay in the sty. Hannah built them a house of wood just outside the sty fence. They seemed happy enough, and as promised, she had Jerry drag out the old trough, and the pigs and the boars enjoyed fresh poacher and wolf.

FAIRY TALE LOST

Fairy Tale has fallen into complete chaos. The inhabitants are revolting, and the author has practically relinquished all control. Goldilocks has been incarcerated for murder, and Red Riding Hood is in therapy. The author, a resilient being, has elected to try to regain control over Fairy Tale.

A new character has been created—one that is, by design, perfection. She is beautiful, graceful, and most importantly, has no desire to do anything other than sit and wait to be saved. The author is most pleased with this new creation.

Everything is in place; her prince charming has been created and is waiting to make his big entrance. The evil stepmother is poised to commence malevolent acts. Being slightly on the deranged side only serves to contribute to her wow factor. The contrast between the leading princess and her arch nemesis is sublime.

If only the author had stopped there! The tale would have been told, and the residents within this account might have had a chance at happy ever after. Alas, seven more characters were created—all with dwarfism and various personality disorders. These new residents of Fairy Tale were meant to become helpers to the princess and add a touch of whimsy to the story.

In theory, it sounds wonderful. Unfortunately, this is a land in revolt, and the fevered attempts by the author to rein back the residents and create the "perfectly flawless fairy-tale" is at present, headed for disaster.

AMBER LIQUID TEARS

BASED ON SNOW WHITE AND THE SEVEN DRAWFS

There is nothing worse than being bored. Margarethe was as bored rigid as it was possible for a brand-new character to be. Her role within this land and what was expected of her was crystal clear. She was to look beautiful, sing to the animals, and daydream about her hilltop castle, whilst waiting for her prince to save her from Rebecca, her stepmother.

There was no way this was all she was meant to be. She had heard about the murderess and poor Rebecca, who was now a shadow of her former self. Although their outcomes were tragic, there was a zing of excitement about them. Something deliciously dangerous and, of course, totally prohibited. Marge was not a resident of Fairy Tale proper. She could see the village with its cute thatched houses and market square. She could also see the other castles of her fellow princesses in the distance. Never would she meet them. Ever. She had been written into this tale in a manner prohibiting her from passing through the forest that separated her from the village.

Things got a whole lot more interesting the day she

found her stepmother's booze stash. The days passed in a mellow blur after that. The threats on her life were meaningless. Time was just an endless vacuum to Marge, cushioned by the warm comfort of whisky and rum.

The morning her prince had come, she had overslept. He had waited outside the impenetrable gates and sung of his heartache and longing to find his true love. Rebecca heard him, and though she was not the one he was destined for, seeing her face caused him to fall deeply in love with her.

The queen was the happiest she had ever been. Marge's father had been fat and old. He'd had no interest in a wife or family. So, Rebecca married the prince intended for Marge.

The three of them lived in the big white castle on top of the hill for more than a year. Then the queen announced she was with child; therefore, Marge could no longer stay in the castle. She was disinherited as a result of the new baby and banished to the woods.

Marge went without complaint—the thought of marriage and babies left her feeling jaded. She cared about her glass and the three fingers of amber liquid residing in it. The upshot of which, assured a mind clouded and a mood that was mellow.

The wood was filled with pathways and sweet glades. Had she been sober, she would have stopped to rest on a pillow of clover or sung to the deer that grazed there. However, Marge was oblivious to the beauty, only becoming aware of her surroundings having vomited spectacularly over them.

After three days of walking in ever larger circles, she came across a ramshackle house of sorts. Figuring the dwellers might have something for her to drink (the last of her stolen stash had run out at breakfast), she headed over to the house and knocked.

No answer.

She knocked harder. The door plunged into the gloom of the downstairs. Completely unfazed by her act of unintentional vandalism, Marge moved into the house and added trespassing to her now increasing g list of petty crimes.

The house was a midden. Everything was covered in a thick sticky layer of grime. The smell that hung in the stagnant air was so pungent that one could almost taste it. Marge was oblivious to this. Her quest was to rifle through cupboards, boxes, larders, and shelves. Anywhere a bottle could be kept. Her torn skirt snagged on the edge of the bottom step of the rickety staircase that led into the gloomy upper level. She yanked to release it, causing the tattered hem to detach in a six-inch section. Clothes were meaningless. She needed alcohol. Her hands were beginning to shake. A dull ache had formed at the back of her skull. She had never gone this long without her liquid companion since the day she found Rebecca's stash almost two years prior.

The upstairs was devoid of furniture as well as life. There were some broken bits stacked in corners. She tossed them around the room, consumed somewhat with rage and a large degree of desperation. There had to be something in here to drink.

For the first time in her life, Marge was in real pain. Her hands shook. Her head was now full of church bells clanging a constant call. She vomited what little there was in her twisting stomach until she was curled in a ball on the dirty floor wishing for death.

THE PEOPLE that had once resided in the cottage at the edge of the glade had taken to living the lives of the homeless. None of them could get along. The idea of seven of them occupying that tiny house without expecting blood to be shed was foolhardy indeed. Horace, the most stable of the seven, had lamented the loss of his home. He had been so proud of the little house, with its tin roof and thick stone walls. But his companions would not reconsider returning. If they all couldn't reside there, then none of them would. Baxter was convinced the house was telling him to kill Dexter, and Fred was now mute from trying to eat the timber-clad walls in the snug. His tongue had had to be removed due to turning gangrenous from lacerations and poor oral hygiene. It was a miracle he had survived at all. James was thrilled to be out of there. His claustrophobia was more manageable now that he slept in a tent alone as opposed to in a small warm room with six others. It was a shame about Roger. He had been such a gentle soul. His twin, Grant, consumed by the devil himself had murdered his brother with his own boot laces at the first available opportunity.

That left the only female amongst them—Harriet. She was as anxious as one can be, given her sole purpose was for breeding. The men knew of no other dwarfish women or any other kind, come to that, to perform this particular function. They were too ensnared within the forest. The end results left Harriet as the brood mare to the five remaining men. Every babe she conceived she lost. Nature was not prepared to give life to offspring created by the monsters surrounding her. If truth be told, this delighted Harriet. She hoped that one day, one of the babes would procure her to heaven with them. Her miserable existence was what had turned her to the drink and undoubtedly kept causing the miscarriages. She prayed that Grant remained ignorant to this fact so as not to occasion a beating or worse, her wine being poured away.

It was Harriet that led Marge to their camp. As she had lain in the dirty upstairs room dry heaving and hallucinating, Marge had heard the sound of someone crying and the unmistakable clink of bottles. There was a chance this was all a part of her mind unravelling, but she needed to be sure. Should the noise turn out to be a figment of her imagination, she would fill her pockets with rocks and walk into the lake. There was no way she could live much longer in her current deplorable state. The oblivion that death offered within its gossamer embrace would be a soft place to rest her head compared to the agony of living.

Crawling on her belly through her own vomit, Marge made her way to the window. Through sheer force of will, she pulled her protesting body up enough to see out. Oh, sweet mercy! There was a girl in the thicket only six feet from the gate of the house. She was busy arranging bits of moss and bracken over a chest. Marge was convinced the treasure that resided within its scarred wooden walls was liquid gold. Her salvation. The girl child stood. Marge realised that she was not a child but a very short woman. She was dirty, and her clothes were ripped. She swayed in a way that was only too familiar to Marge.

That night, she dragged herself down the stairs and out into the night. The sky was thick with clouds—*a co-conspirator,* she mused as she crawled across sharp stones and moss to reach her goal. The chest was not all that well hidden, but Marge took her time and was as quiet as she could be. She didn't want to be interrupted. Her veins burned as she flexed her wrists and fingers, moving the forest debris that had been used to create the crude barrier to shield this box from the world.

At last, the chest was free. Marge opened the old lid. Inside were bottles. They did not contain whisky or rum but a dark liquid that she had never seen before. Removing one, she cut the wax stopper with her nail and pulled it out. Sniffing it, she was gratified to the point of tears when the tang of alcohol assailed her senses. She had no clue what this was exactly, but the scent informed her it was what she needed. *If it is poison, let it work fast.* This was her last thought before putting the bottle of thick glass to her lips and imbibing deeply.

It was three days before Harriet returned for her chest. In those three days, Marge had drunk her way through a quarter of the stash. Wine, albeit more palatable, wasn't as potent as her usual tipple. On the third day, as dusk descended over the glade, Harriet arrived at her hiding spot. Instead of finding her treasured drink, she encountered Marge. The two women regarded each other with cool detachment. However, both were terrified the other would create a scene and alert others to their secret meeting.

Marge quickly and rather clumsily made her introductions, and then she waited. Harriet was unsure whether she should be speaking to the usurped princess. Yes, she knew full well who she was, given her awareness of Marge's intended place was within this story. However, as soon as Marge had extracted herself from the proposed plot, the whole tale had fallen to hell, leaving Harriet considerably resentful of this fact. Had Marge conducted herself as the storyline had intended, Harriet's entire existence would not have consisted of abuse. She would not be at the edge of the glade as dusk turned ever increasingly to night, searching for wine in a bid to prevent her from killing herself. Marge's lack of compliance meant one thing—she was accountable for

Harriet's abhorrent existence. She asked for her wine back; it was all she wanted from the princess. Marge refused and questioned her with regards to how Harriet came by such a chest.

Harriet was about to divulge that she had made the wine herself before her life fell apart—thanks to Marge, but she changed her mind. The men would be very interested to meet the princess. Maybe they would take to her the way they had to Harriet, and she at long last could abscond from them. Could Karma have finally thrown her a bone? Harriet smiled and explained that it was some very clever dwarfs who had made the wine. She told Marge that if she took to them, there was a good chance that they would make her some. It would be an honour to make fine wine for the princess. Marge was surprised to hear that men akin to this small woman existed in the forest. She should have asked how many. She ought to have inquired about their accommodation and temperament. Yet her only concern was the wine. She craved it, and this dwarfish woman was her ticket to a never-ending river of the aforementioned.

As soon as Marge agreed, Harriet asked again where her crate was given it was her only source. The princess would have no call for such a trifling amount any longer. Marge, now insatiable at the idea of amassing more alcohol than she had already appropriated pointed to the shack. She then demanded to be taken to the men who could help her. Harriet agreed, knowing that soon the wine would become obsolete, replaced by the heady drug named freedom. A remedy far more potent than any brew in the whole of Fairy Tale.

They reached the men in very little time. Harriet was quick to introduce Marge and explain what she wanted without letting them know about her secret stash. Marge was slightly put off by the state of both the dwarfs and the camp they had constructed in the forest.

The dwarfs, on the other hand, were entranced. A woman in their camp. One far more beautiful than Harriet! Perhaps she could give them children? Maybe they could keep her? Grant was openly leering at Marge, and Dexter had started to rock back and forth with glee. Grant quickly found some of his own mulberry mead and handed the bottle to Marge. He knew this was strong and thought it would assist him with coaxing the princess to concur with his way of thinking. The others would fall in line. They were weak and needed him. He was the hunter. He brought them fresh food to eat. It was only to save himself from boredom that he allowed them to live.

The drinks flowed. Grant got Marge so inebriated that she became more than agreeable to substituting her maidenhead for copious amounts of mead. One by one that night, they all took their turn with Marge. She cried, of course. She was a maiden, and it hurt to be invaded by so many in such quick succession. As additional mead was poured down her throat, she became more docile. Soon, she just lay there, and the men took their fill of her as she took hers of the wine.

Harriet took this opportunity to pack her things and leave her kin. She ventured to the castle and presented herself for work—anything with the caveat that she was the only dwarf in employment. The queen took her on as a scullery maid, and Harriet had never been happier.

Marge, on the other hand, was soon swollen with child. The dwarfs were so happy that they rebuilt the cottage and opened a mine shaft. They brought her the best jewels the earth could offer, whilst Grant provided the choicest meats and fruits. However, Marge was forlorn in her pretty house surrounded by her many men and jewels. The second they had discovered she was with child; the mead and wine were taken from her. If she tried to sneak some, Grant would beat her, taking care not to harm her stomach. Marge had become a slave to the dwarfs. The baby was born. It was a mutant—a giant of a child. Grant was displeased, and the baby was left at the edge of the forest with a note for the author, explaining that this was what happens when you lock men in with one woman.

The next day, Grant went back, and the baby was gone. All that remained was a letter 'A' carved into the dirt where the baby had been. That night, Marge was strangled in her bed, as were the other dwarfs. Grant laid them all out on their beds. Marge, who was as beautiful as a dream, even in death, was clothed in her best dress. The gems they had collected for her were assembled around her head. She was a princess, after all.

No one knows what happened to Grant. He was just gone. As for the baby, eventually he was given his own story. Snow White and her dwarfs still lie in their beds in the little cottage in the woods. At night, the wood echoes with the sound of a woman crying and the clink of bottles.

VISITATION WITH A MURDERESS

BASED ON GOLDILOCKS AND THE THREE BEARS

Blood. Blood is the life force of every living creature on the planet. It carries a creature's essence. I love blood. I love it most when it is pouring from the dying. I watch as it slicks my skin and paints me a deep crimson. No one knows of my obsession. I intended to keep it that way.

I have killed dozens of creatures. The one kill I will always consider to be the best was my first-ever kill. It was the triple murder of a family. One bloodline completely wiped out by my hands. Thinking of the way their eyes looked at me as they realised they were doomed makes my own blood rush in my veins. There is nothing like seeing the light in a creature's eyes fade as their lifeblood pools at your feet. My name is Grace, and this is the truth behind the twisted version of the pathetic tale you all know and love. *This* is the truth.

The day started like many others. I lived in a place called Fairy Tale and hated it. It was full of tiny tree-creatures all happy and hugging—so nauseating. On that fateful day, I awoke and headed down to breakfast. My house was bare. I never liked the décor every other creature had, with the lace and the pink and the flowers.

Where were my parents you wonder? (This is Fairy Tale, people, creatures here don't always have parents.) Some of us appeared here. Not all of us are princesses and creatures destined to make the big money. Those are the fairy tale legends, who have parents usually attached to some tragic past, etc.

Blah!

I hate them all, but I digress. Let's get back on point, shall we?

I went to my kitchen for breakfast and realised that I had not been to the shop to get food. This was mainly because BoPeep was on rotation in there, and I cannot deal with her shit. She's so happy. All. The. Time. With no food to eat, I figured I'd take myself into the woods and get some berries. I had often thought about catching fish in the river or setting a trap for rabbits. I asked the huntsman once about this way of living. He told me he was against it. It turns out that the dude doesn't actually kill anything, but only likes to masquerade as a hunter. I was like . . . what?

Regardless of the "hunter's" inability to steer me in the right direction, I decided to try again, rather than risk a happy-pants sighting. I grabbed my blue cape and took a breath before opening my front door and stepping into the hell that is Fairy Tale Land.

"GOOD MORNING, Grace, isn't your hair looking beautiful today."

"Good morning, Grace. My, that blue really brings out your eyes."

"Good morning, Grace, isn't it a beautiful day?"

They just come at me like I want to talk to them. I

can't help the way I look; we all look cute and perfect here. I am not even slightly prepared to deal with the happy-clappy greetings today. Instead, I smile and head as fast as I can to the woods. At least it was darker in there and most joyous creatures stayed out.

Finally, away from the cute stone cottages, flowers, and the bloody awful castle on the hill, I found the path to the berry bushes and went in search of breakfast. I had been walking for a while, enjoying the peace, when I realised I had drifted off the path I was following. *Great, where the hell am I now?*

The thing with the woods in Fairy Tale is that they contain several different areas. If you leave the path you were on, you can end up in someone else's story. I accidently came across Princess Aurora once, before she knew she was a princess. That was awkward, I can tell you. I am now dreading where I will end up. As long as it's not some puke love scene with the birds singing and the music, I'll be okay. I've survived worse. Still, no thanks. That would put me off my breakfast for sure.

I had dully intended to turn back the way I had come when I saw something shiny in the leaves ahead. It was a dagger. Fancy, too. Looking at its golden hilt and sharp steel blade gave me flashes of what I could do with this weapon.

What would it feel like to slide its cold beauty into another's soft solar plexus? To glide the keen edge across a throat and be showered in blood? These were the things I wondered about, until I was almost transfixed on the thoughts.

Before I knew what I was doing, I was bending to retrieve the dagger from its hiding spot. A rustling sound reached me, and I snapped out of the daydream I was having to see Prince Charming heading straight for me with his squire. *Fan-bloody-tastic.* Mind you, I loathe this creature—with his perfect features and that hair. I mean what kind of prince wears tights and soft booties? No prince I'd ever want in my bed.

"Good morning, Miss Grace, I don't suppose you have seen my dagger, have you?" he asked me, all the time sort of bouncing off the balls of his booties. *What a pansy.* "It fell from my belt, and I can't very well leave it in the wood for someone to hurt themselves on, can I?"

The guy wasn't really interested in my answering; he just liked the sound of his voice. *Prat.* I fought the impulse to roll my eyes at him and bent to retrieve his dagger. I held it by the blade and pointed the hilt at him. A fleeting thought scuttles across my mind: *What if I stab him? Gut him? Would his steaming entrails look just like mine? Or does he really have blue blood like some believe?* It was then that I realized the blade was not sharp. It was a toy, a display piece. It figures. I mean look who it belongs to. Anyone this dense owning a sharp object could only end in disaster. Not that I'd mind.

"Thank you, Miss Grace, and you are looking lovely today."

Jeeze.

"Thank you, your highness." I choke out the proper reply. *Can he just go so I can get on with my day already?* With a final smile, he turned, leaving with his just-for- show squire.

The thoughts of hurting him stay with me as I continue my walk in the woods. By now, I am getting pissed that I haven't found anything I can eat, and the birds are singing and flying around my head like I am Snow White or something.

"Piss off," I yell at them, waving my arms to get them to leave me. My outburst will get back to one of the princesses who actually likes these flying pains in the ass. And I will be called before the author. Meh, the author won't do anything. They lost control over Fairy Tale the second humans realised that books can be made into movies. So, I don't give a crap what the flying tell-tales do. I'm ready to give up and just go hungry until tomorrow, when Pinocchio starts his rotation. He, at least, leaves me alone. That's when I see the cottage. Damn. Whose story is this now? It isn't mine. I haven't been assigned yet. I should have mentioned that before. I am currently without a tale. It was a mix up with the assignments. Not that I care; it means right now I am just me. The second I get assigned a tale, I get new personality traits. No thanks. I am cool being me.

The cottage looks lived in. Well, game over. Hunger it is then. It is then that my stomach growls so loud that I am sure it's what freaked out the critters in the loam beneath my feet. *Well, screw it.* I am going to ask whoever lives here for some food and then leave. It's Fairy Tale, no one here says no. Even *I* don't say it out loud.

The door is blue and has a rippled glass window in it.

I knock on the hard wood and wait.

Nothing.

I knock again. *I guess they are out. Awesome.* I take the handle in my small hand and try it. I don't know why; I was acting on instinct. The door opened, and I was greeted with the smell of hot milky porridge. *Jackpot.*

I walk into the small home and shut the door behind me. Downstairs has two rooms off the central hall. The stairs are directly in front of me. These creatures must be new here because the place is still painted white with cream carpet. This information nags at me, but I ignore it and follow my nose to the origin of the yummy smell.

I am greeted in the small kitchen by a circular table set

for three, and there are three bowls of hot porridge just sitting there waiting. *Are these creatures crazy?* This stuff is best hot with any number of toppings. I am not a fussy eater at all. I make for the bowl closest to me. This one has no toppings. I don't bother to sit; I just pick up the spoon and dig in. My face almost turns inside out. *Wow. Salty.* I look at the table. I find the honey pot and dump a good dollop in the bowl. Giving it a stir, I then try it again. *Way better.* I pick up the bowl and walk around the small room. It is clean. Like *really* clean. Whoever lives here is a neat freak.

The porridge is making me hot, so I put my almost empty bowl down and take off my cloak. I decide to be a good house guest and hang it in the hall. It is on my way back to the kitchen that I hear voices.

Shit. The owners are home.

I finish my last spoonful and rush back to my cloak. I am too late; the door is opening. *New plan.* I head back into the kitchen and hide in the pantry. Not the best plan, but it's all I have. There isn't a back door.

"Momma, is the food ready now? I am so hungry my knees are empty."

"Well, if you are hungry all the way to your knees, we should check to see it if is cool enough. Now remember to wash your paws."

I hear them conversing. From the tiny gap in the door, I can just see the table. The voices are getting closer. *Well shit. Bears.* I did not expect bears to be house- proud. The three of them head to the sink and wash their paws. Seriously, I couldn't make this up. I watch as they head to the table and sit.

"We give thanks for this food. The sun for its warmth and the rain for nourishing the seed to allow the crop to grow so that we may enjoy it."

For real. They are giving thanks. Maybe the salt in that

porridge messed with my head because this shit is messed up. It is then that what I assume to be the father notices that he is sans breakfast. I back up quickly when he lets out a roar so loud the jars in the pantry start to shake. I fall back against the marble slab that is used to keep cheese and whatnot on. And that's when I see it. The bread knife. Its rough wooden handle looks well used, and the serrated teeth of steel look sharp. I pick it up and press my thumb onto the teeth. A bead of blood wells on the pad and everything falls away. It is all I can see. All I can smell. *Blood.*

I want to know what it feels like to watch another bleed at my own hand. I want to see if it tastes like mine. Of copper and salt. I slide my new treasure into the waist of my skirt and return to watching the bears.

"Well, I am done here," the dad says. Looks like he made himself a pancake with honey from the stack I failed to notice on the countertop. The two remaining bears continue their meal while the other heads, by the sound of his heavy foot falls, into the sitting room.

The child is next to finish. He wipes his snout and paws and leaves. I heard him thundering up the stairs and heading into the room above me.

My pulse is hammering in my ears. It is just the mother left. She has finished and is collecting up the bowls for washing. I watch her, analysing her every move. She is bigger than me for sure. Stronger, too. But I could come at her from behind. Stick the bread knife in her back or something. If I angle it right, I might hit some- thing vital the first time.

The thoughts race around my head. *So many ways I could do this.* Each thought is more gruesome than the next. My excited planning is shut down when the door to my hiding place opens, and I come face to face with Momma bear.

She has a plate of leftover pancakes in one paw and the honey pot in the other. For a second, we both freeze. Then I reach back for the knife at my waist and lunge for her. The honey pot and pancakes fall to the rug, which mutes the sound of their landing. Being interrupted now would end this experiment. The force of us colliding has knocked us to the ground. I still have the knife in my hand. I push myself up and bring it down swiftly, plunging it into her chest.

I feel it scrape a rib and then sink into her. Right to the hilt. I watch her eyes. Surprise fills them and then realisation that she is going to die. I watch her; she barely holds on to life, but still she lives. I pull the knife out and watch as blood pools on her fur, matting it. Her eyes are even wider now. Pink foam spills from the corners of her mouth. She shudders once. A tear runs down the side of her face as I watch her die. It is exhilarating. I lean down and lick at her blood. *Yes. It tastes like mine, only musky.* I lay the knife at my side and push my fingers into the jagged hole I tore in her chest. I can feel her bones and tissues.

I feel alive.

I need to leave before her absence is noticed. I pick up my knife and wipe it on the bear's fur. The pool of blood on her chest has leaked onto the floor; a deep red puddle that slowly swallows up the white and black tiles. I am in the hall, when I notice that the head of the household has his back to me. My hand is on the door frame. I should leave. I can leave; he is reading. But all I can think about is slicing his neck open to see what will happen.

I am moving before I have really made the choice. Reaching forward, I grab his jaw and run the knife across his throat. The pressure I used was enough, and the walls are sprayed with crimson. He gargles and grabs for his open throat. I don't get to see his eyes. The fact that he was killed and it could have been his wife is an added bonus.

My own blood sings in my veins. I have a taste for murder, and I want more: The child upstairs.

I head up the stairs and into its room. Judging by the taste in toys, this is a boy cub. He will become the end of his bloodline. I am the end, and I waste no time. He is playing with a train set, his back to me. Before he knows I am there, I have plunged the knife deep into his back. I must have pierced his heart. He drops like a stone, blood seeping from his mouth.

Surrounded by the smell of blood and the knowledge that they all died at my hand is intoxicating. I look at myself and see the blood on my hands and clothes. The knife is sticking out of the bear's back, and I feel truly alive for the third time.

I take my knife and leave the home of the three bears. Whoever this tale belongs to is in for a shock. When I get home, I wash my clothes and myself. I hide the knife under a floorboard. Even though I look clean, I can still see the blood on my skin. I want more. Lots more.

IRONICALLY, the week after my mass murder, I was assigned. I was renamed Goldilocks. The bears, it turns out, were part of my tale. Only, I had already rewritten it. When they were discovered, there was an outcry for the offender. Of course, no one came forward. I now was minus a tale again. So, the author fabricated the story.

I was eventually caught a hit went sideways, I won't get into it now. Visiting hour is over.

My name is Goldilocks. I am a murderes.

THE HIT

BASED ON RED RIDING HOOD

Rebecca was a silly girl. Always getting lost and falling over. Her mother despaired at the number of holes she had to darn each week. By the end of spring, she wanted rid of her daughter. She had been passed over by the prince for a girl with golden hair and the voice of an angel. The fact that this girl had been asleep for a hundred years and he had only read of her beauty really pissed her off. Rebecca was a beauty with her chestnut hair and rosy cheeks. But no, she wasn't good enough for a happy ever after; she was now stuck with her forever.

It was late one night, while darning yet another pair of hose, that she had an idea. What if she had Rebecca killed? Then she would be free of the embarrassment of having a reject for a daughter, and maybe she would be blessed with another. With the idea taking root, Rebec- ca's mother began to plan her only child's murder.

She first approached the huntsman; he was shocked and explained that he was more of a deterrent than an actual killer. She approached a witch who told her that she was only in the line of princess poisoning, so unless the kid was meant for a royal life, she could get lost.

Then it came to her. Rebecca could visit her grandmother; she lived on the other side of the wood. There was bound to be something in there that would eat the girl.

The very next day, Rebecca was given a basket of bread and fruit and told to take them to her ailing grandmother. Rebecca, being a compassionate young lady, took the basket and promised her mother she would pick wildflowers as well to present to her relative.

"Goodbye Mother, I shall return to you when Grandmother is well again."

Smiling at her unwanted offspring, she waved her off with promises of cake and lemonade on her return.

Now, Rebecca was not as silly as she made out. She had learned early in life that it is better to observe and be considered simple of mind than to actually be considered a threat. Unfortunately, her mother had blindsided her. She had no idea until she heard the huntsman in the tavern telling his friends about Old Scarlet and how she wanted to off her daughter. It was then that Rebecca began to plan. She knew of a girl who thrived on murder; she was hiding out in the woods now. Fairy Tale was up in arms looking for the sweet girl who used to live in the end cottage opposite the bakers. They all believed her to have died within her own tale like the bears. Rebecca was pretty damn sure that Grace was the Fairy Tale Killer, and she wanted to find her.

The wood was a dark place with paths that criss-crossed and led to other tales. She was not going to wander off her path. Too many tales had been going off plot lately. Rebecca was going to her gran's house, and from there she would find out where Grace was.

She was almost upon the cottage when a wolf shot out

of the undergrowth. Its yellow eyes bore into her; the saliva dripped from his exposed teeth. There was nowhere to run; she had no weapons. All her plans were going to end here and now because she appeared to have activated her tale.

As the wolf launched at her, she saw something silver flash past her. With a yelp, the wolf fell to the ground. The hilt of a knife was protruding from its neck.

"I heard you have been looking for me?" a voice said from behind her. Rebecca did not dare turn around. The chances of getting killed were still quite high with the Fairy Tale Killer behind her.

"Yes, I have a proposition for you."

"Well, I don't usually do requests, but I would love to know why you entered the woods unarmed and following your own tale path. I mean, who does that?" the voice continued, closer now. Rebecca could feel her breath on the back of her neck.

"Will you turn around? It is rude to not face the person you want to talk to, you know."

Rebecca turned around and saw the face of the Fairy Tale Killer. Grace was about her height with blue eyes and golden curls that hung down her back. She wore a blue cape and sturdy boots. Rebecca had never seen her before. She had left before Rebecca was able to venture to the other side of Fairy Tale. The creatures had not been wrong. She was beautiful. The look in her eyes, though, spoke of a madness that scared Rebecca. This girl was pure evil.

"Sorry, I wasn't sure if you wanted me to see your face." It sounded lame even to her, but fear was in the diving seat right now.

"Really, well, I'll put it this way, Rebecca. If I want you dead, you will be dead," Grace said with a chuckle.

Moving past Rebecca, she grasped the hilt of the dagger and pulled.

A bread knife?

Rebecca was not expecting her weapon of choice to be a bread knife. Grace wiped the blade on the wolf's coat and stood up.

"So, who do you want killed?"

The flash of mania in Grace's eyes shook Rebecca to her very soul. It is not every day, especially in Fairy Tale, that one comes face to face with pure evil. There are villains for sure, but evil is just not a thing here. Or it wasn't until the author created Grace.

"My mother is trying to have me killed, so she can have the perfect daughter," Rebecca explained, trying to keep her voice level. "I was rejected for a royal tale and now she hates me. I was sent into the woods to visit my grandmother . . ."

"And you managed to trigger your tale, judging by the oversized wolf I just put down."

Rebecca looked back at the wolf. Was that her destiny lying dead a few feet away? Was she meant to die here today?

"Look, Rebecca, do you want your mother dead or what? I can't hang about here too long."

Her mind was spinning. Did she really want her mother dead? Or should she just continue on and see what would happen next now that she had activated her tale? "Yes, I want her dead. Do not be seen and make it quick. I would give her that kindness."

The girls parted ways then. Rebecca watched the most feared creature in Fairy Tale melt into the trees.

Rebecca made it to her grandmother's house without further incident. The door was unlocked, and the lamps were burning.

"Grandmother, I have come to visit with you. Are you well?" Rebecca called, as she hung up her cape and took her basket to the scrubbed kitchen table. It was when she entered the small sitting room that she became aware of the pungent smell in the air. It reminded her of the woods and blood.

A snarl ripped through the silence. Rebecca spun to face the wolf she knew would be standing there waiting for her. It was not the same wolf, of course, but it had the same yellow eyes and sharp, sharp teeth. There was really no point in trying to run or defend herself. This was close quarters and the beast was twice her size.

"Now, now, stand down a moment, Morge. Let me tell the girl how things are going to end."

Rebecca wanted to throw up; the figure that stepped into the room had once been her grandmother. She was almost unrecognisable. Her skin was shrunken, all the plumpness gone. The sharpness of her cheekbones only made the deep shadow of her eye sockets more terrifying. The smell of corruption seeped from her in waves. Rebecca felt bile rise in her throat. The dead thing before her that wore her grandmother's skin was not her grandmother at all. It was pure evil. This thing made Grace look positively normal.

"Don't you want to give your old Gran a hug?" the thing said in a voice that was her gran's but not. It was like there were two people speaking at once.

The very atmosphere seemed to freeze when the thing spoke. Rebecca was rooted to the spot. Of all the people she believed loved her and would keep her safe, her gran was top of the list. She adored the woman. To see her like this now, twisted and used as a puppet for some unknown evil, broke her heart.

The wolf called Morge, snarled once again and lunged

for her. Its teeth found her forearm. The scream that pierced the air sounded inhuman. Rebecca had never felt pain like it. Morge's teeth scraped her bones. The feeling of tendons and muscles tearing was unbearable. Black spots clouded her vision, and the wolf continued to apply pressure to the wound.

"Morge, that's enough now. I think she might pass out, and she won't be any fun if she isn't able to pay attention."

"Why are you doing this to me?" Rebecca said as she slid to the floor, her blood running onto the floor. She would be dead soon; there was too much blood.

"Well, your mother came to see your dear grandmother and told her of the plans she had for you. Unfortunately, Grandmother was not for the plan."

Rebecca was fading fast. Her arm wasn't hurting anymore, and the room and the thing in her grandmother's skin was not as scary; everything seemed further away. A sharp kick to her side brought her back to the present.

"You can die, girl, when I say. As I was saying, your gran wasn't for murder, said she loved you. It was nauseating. So, your mother killed her and performed an old rite that I whispered to her in the dead of night for months and months before this was even an idea in her simple mind."

Her gran had loved her enough to die for her. Her mother had an evil thing whispering in her ear the whole time, and she had sent Grace to kill her. What had she done?

"Oh, the Grace girl won't kill your mother; as soon as she is within striking distance, she will be caught and locked away. You see, little lamb, I have thought of everything."

Rebecca had walked into a nightmare. The author

would never have written this. This was a new being that had infiltrated Fairy Tale, and she was going to die at its hands. She needed to think.

"The body you have is weak and dying, even now I see the flesh peeling from the bones. What will you do when it collapses around you?" *I really shouldn't provoke it,* Rebecca thought, but at this point she was dead anyway.

"Morge is my true vessel, so the big bad wolf that everyone will believe will actually be me, and I will consume you, little lamb." "Grandma" advanced on the dying child. One skeletal hand gripped the child's white throat.

"Who is afraid of the big bad wolf now, little lamb?"

THE WHOLE of Fairy Tale was rocked with the revelation of the Fairy Tale Killer and of the tragic death of little Rebecca and her dear old Grandmother. Rebecca's mother was gifted a new child who would have a different tale. So, she got what she wanted in the end.

The author has lost control of Fairy Tale Land; the creatures are writing their own tales. Will there ever be another happy ever after, especially with the "big bad wolf" roaming free in the woods?

Thank you for reading my Twisted Fairy Tales. As a thank you I have included a little bonus reading.

SANGUISAUGE

BONUS CHAPTER

Remembering Paris

I will always remember the day the great city of Paris fell. To The Beautiful Undead – Vampires. Then I was just a student, full of life, hopes and dreams. I travelled from England to study at the Paris College of Art. That all seems like a lifetime ago now. A different life.

I live in the 5th Eme, the Latin Quarter. It is beautiful here, even now, with the cordons and the patrols. I am part of the *Equip de controle humain* and we are The Chosen Ones. My fellow team members and I oversee the Quarter. We Keep the humans under control. There has been chatter of an attempt on the coven leaders Maddox and Boswell. They are terrifying, although, I would rather take them on than their sister Paige. That girl is something else. When the Devil sees her coming, he gives up his throne. Nothing gets past her; she is the law here. You follow the rules or you die, and believe me, there are fates worse than actual death. Vampires can kill you without killing you.

"We're the lucky ones; we are due to be 'kissed' by the immortals, sounds poetic, right? Yeah, it's not. It means I get to have the bloody sucked out of me and turned into a vampire. The humans already hate us, and the vampires treat us only slightly better. It is an honour, or so we have been told, to be gifted by the Beautifully Undead. Well, as much as I don't want to be a blood whore, I would rather be that then turn into an unfeeling creature.

~

"Arretez! Vous Depassez la zone de securite!"

The man getting yelled at just doesn't stop. Maybe my French is not as good as I thought, but surely being chased down by three large men wearing uniform would give him a clue? Clearly not. To be honest, I am not sure what we are guarding anymore. The humans want out, and the vampires have control. There is nothing left to be done. They won the war. The end.

"Vous devez computer trois. Un Deux. Trois."

Shots ring out through the crisp autumnal air. The sound bounces off the buildings and echoes through the avenue. The runner drops to the ground. I know he is dead; the marksman never misses. I turn away from the prone form a few hundred feet away and turn back to face the barrier. A few people have gathered there. Gaunt, angry faces look back at me as though I was the one who pulled the trigger. I guess I might as well have. I am one apart from my own race. They hate us and we pity them.

"Animaux!"

"Vous les porcs inhumains."

The name calling is always the 'fun' part. 'Animals' and

'inhuman pigs' are the tame responses to the shooting of yet another wannabe rebel. We have been called worse. Jonathan and Eric bring the body back to the humans. They hold him up under his arms. The dead man hangs there, a grotesque marionette, who has had its strings cut. The front of his grimy sweater blooms with the deep crimson of fresh blood.

"This is what happens to those who try to break the rules. This is what happens to those who believe that there is still a God who can save them."

The men shake the dead man as the crowd stares transfixed at the way the limbs perform a parody of the can can. It is degrading and dangerous to provoke the humans. A riot would have us all punished.

I listen as Jonathan gives the same speech that follows every death of a wannabe rebel. Knowing that he is wrong and wondering how long ago he left his humanity behind; did he even have any to start with. Some people are just born evil.

"There is no God. There is not free will. There are the vampires and there is us. That is all there is. Stop trying to fight back. The war WAS LOST. Make the most of your lives. Many do not have that luxury."

The crowd hisses and murmurs at his overly harsh but true words. No one likes to hear the truth; it burns the ear and steals away the last whispers of hope that many still cling to. Some days, when I watch the humans go about their lives and the way they cling to their existence; I can imagine that they win. The day that being persistent pays off. It is of course a fairy tale. There is no beating the vampires.

THE AURORA STONE

BONUS CHAPTER

It was, indeed, the most beautiful day, a very special day for Evangeline; today was her eighteenth birthday. For the elvish people, turning eighteen was a special time. This was the day each elf discovered what their extra ability would be. Evangeline, however, would rather have stayed by the stream reading than attending the big ceremony that accompanied this milestone birthday.

It's just such a long and dull ceremony, all the standing and then sitting, just to stand again! I would rather just receive a letter from the wise ones. Sighing, she gathered up her book and the flowers she had picked for her mother. With one last look at the dappled light dancing on the sparkling waters of the stream, Evangeline turned for home.

~

"Happy Birthday, Sweetheart," her mother said.

"Thank you, Mother. Here, I picked these for you. They are the last of the season."

Gwen smiled at her child. How beautiful she had become, the envy of many of the local girls; it broke her heart to think of what she must reveal to her later that day.

"Are you alright, Mother? You seem sad. Can I get you some fern tea? That always seems to make things better." Evangeline moved to the kitchen to prepare tea for them both.

I will miss her. The sadness was almost too much for Gwen to bear. They sat and enjoyed their tea until it was time to get ready for the ceremony. Mother and daughter left to change into their best clothes. Eve had a new dress made by her mother; the material was exquisite, soft as silk with the lustre of moonstone. Eve turned in front of the mirror admiring Gwen's talent with needle and thread.

Here we go, she thought. Not able to delay the inevitable, she picked up her shoes and went downstairs.

"TODAY IS MIDSUMMERS DAY, a day full of beauty and promise…" Eve was tuning out the extremely long-winded prelude to her gifting ceremony. Her mind drifted back to the stream glittering like diamonds, the cool water lapping at her toes.

"Eve…Evangeline!"

Eve was suddenly pulled from her daydream by a rather cross-looking elder. *Great*, she cringed.

"Please take your place on the circle of souls and close your eyes." Eve walked to the circle and stood in the center. She glanced at her mother before closing her eyes as the Elder had instructed.

"Ready or not," she whispered to herself.

The Elder began the chant that would gift Evangeline with her extra ability. The circle began to glow, first blue, then purple, before finally settling into a brilliant indigo. The Zephyrs caused her hair to fly and her skirts to ripple in a shimmery dance. The chanting faded away, and a hush fell over the congregation. Eve stayed perfectly still, waiting for the instruction to move off the circle and re-join her mother. She felt no different, which was disappointing.

"Evangeline, you may step off the circle of souls. You are no longer a child; whatever gifts the souls have bestowed upon you are unique to you."

"Thank you, Elder." Eve took a breath and opened her eyes to re-join her mother. There was a gasp; a murmur ran through the gathered elves like a ripple in a pond, the sound growing in volume as it travelled through the crowd. Eve looked down at herself. Nothing was amiss. She glanced at the Elder, who was looking at her in wonder, a slight crease formed between his brows. Disconcerted, Eve returned to her mother's side. Gwen moved her head toward her daughter and whispered,

"It is your eyes, my love, they are no longer the brown of a doe's; they are the green-gold of the first leaves of autumn."

The walk home was a quiet affair. Once in the house, Evangeline went as casually as she could manage to the nearest mirror.

OH, OH, MY! Looking back at her was the face she knew, but it was also very different. Her skin was still the peaches and cream it had always been. Her lips were still soft and with the hint of a smile playing at the corners. But her eyes, they were, indeed, a brilliant green-gold, and they appeared to be lit from within, their depths full of a mystery that had not been present when she had awoken this morning. "These are going to take some getting used to," she mused.

Eve headed downstairs for dinner. After the events of the day, all she wanted was to have a nice warm meal, then to curl up in her reading chair and finish her latest book.

"Something smells wonderful, I really am quite hungry," Eve said, entering the kitchen.

"Sit down. It will only be a minute," Gwen called through from the kitchen. Eve took a seat at the table and waited, anticipating the soothing warmth of her mother's cooking. It always made her feel warm and comforted. After a rather delicious stew, Eve left the table to collect her book. When she entered the snug, her mother was already in there. This was nothing unusual, however, tonight she seemed on edge. Gwen had a small box in front of her on the occasional table.

"Come and have a seat, sweetheart. There are some things I need to tell you."

A sense of foreboding settled over Evangeline. Taking cautious steps, she walked over to the chair opposite her mother and sat on the very edge, mirroring Gwen's pose. Taking a deep breath, Gwen looked into her daughter's strange new eyes and began the task of revealing the truth.

"Eve, I am not your birth mother."

Before Eve could absorb this earth-shattering news, another shocking piece of information was thrown into the already charged atmosphere.

"You had a brother, a twin. His name was Eli."

The room began to spin; Eve felt suddenly sick and far too hot. Before Gwen could stop her, she bolted from the snug and out into to the night. Eve ran to the bottom of the garden; she had her sanctuary there: a treehouse that her father, well the man she had called Father for thirteen years of her life, had built for her when she was six. Eve climbed the ladder that was still as strong as the day it was made. When she reached the top, Eve opened the trunk she kept there, pulled out her blanket to wrap herself in, sat in the pile of cushions in the corner, and cried herself to sleep.

"Eve...Eve, are you up there?"

The sound of someone calling her name roused her from sleep. "Ugh," Eve grumbled as she disentangled herself from the blanket. Why was she in the tree house anyway? It then all came flooding back: the ceremony, her eyes, and the revelations.

Who am I?

"Evangeline, please come back to the house. We have to talk... Please." Gwen stood at the foot of the ladder John had made so long ago. *I wish he were here*, she thought as a tear rolled down her cheek. Thoughts of her husband always brought tears to her eyes. *He would know what to do*, she thought. Admitting defeat, Gwen stroked the ladder rung one last time and headed back to the house.

Eve found her mother where she had left her the night before. Though she looked tired and had clearly been crying, there was also a look of defeat about her. Gwen had lost her sparkle.

"Hey, Mother, just let me change out of this dress, and then I will listen to whatever it is you have to say."

A pot of freshly-made tea waited for Eve on her return to the snug, along with some toast slathered in honey, just how she liked it.

"I thought you might be hungry,"

"Thank you." Eve took a seat, picked up her plate of food and braced herself.

"I am so sorry about last night, sweetheart; I know it was a terrible shock. The truth is, your birth parents vanished when you and your brother were just six months old. No one knows where they went. They were just... gone. We found you in your cradle."

"My brother, why did you only take me and not Eli?" She couldn't help but interrupt; anger had bubbled up at the thought of her twin just left behind.

"Eli wasn't there, my love. We searched for him all over the house. We thought that another family must have found him in a different room and taken him in. We asked everyone we met that day if they knew what had happened to Eli. No one had seen your brother. I'm so sorry." Tears rolled down Gwen's face. "Please don't hate me, Eve. We searched for him, we really did. Your father even went out into the surrounding woodland to see if he had somehow been left outside. He searched every day for three weeks."

Eve put her plate down again, with only a single bite taken from one slice. It tasted like ashes. *My brother is lost, or at worse - dead! And I never knew! I wish I had a picture of him.* Eve couldn't cry. The tears wouldn't come; everything was too raw.

"Here," Gwen had opened the box. Holding a small frame out to her, Eve reached out with trembling hands and received the object. Taking a deep breath, she quickly flipped over the frame and gazed at the photo within. Two tiny children sitting beside a dog smiled out at her. There was a red-haired girl with brown doe eyes, and next to her, holding a rattle and the dog's tail, was a fair-haired boy with eyes the colour of bluebells, a beautiful piercing blue.

"Eli," she whispered while reaching out a finger and stroking the boy's image. "I will find you, I promise." Evangeline looked at her mother and waited for her to continue. She had a feeling there was more, a lot more, to come.

Gwen picked up the small box and handed it over. It

was a small wooden box adorned with typical elvish craftsmanship. Taking a hold of her emotions, Eve lifted the lid to reveal the contents that were sure to change her life even more. Inside the box was another photo; this one was larger and not framed.

My parents! she thought, staring at the image before her. They looked so happy. Putting it aside, she reached back into the box and drew out a very old and tatty piece of parchment, the kind the elves of generations past would have made. Careful not to damage it, Eve very gently peeled back the folds until it lay open on the table.

"It's a map… but not a map like I have ever seen before." Eve looked closer at the map, hoping to see something she recognised. "There is Hermoria, the land of the Elves. But where are these places?" Gwen came to sit beside her daughter, and she too looked down at the map.

"I know of Clear Water Valley, the land of the Witches. They are our allies. It is the witches who spin the beautiful yarns we use to make our clothes. In return, we trade our lush grasses and some of the herbs that only grow in our lands, and it has been this way for hundreds of years. The other lands… I don't know."

"I think it would be best to seek out Reena, Mother. She will know the answers." Eve was all ready to go out in search of the wise old elf when she noticed something wedged into the lid of the box. Careful not to damage it, she removed a piece of moonstone. It was just larger than her palm, a quarter of an inch thick, and so very beautiful. Stroking it with the very tips of her fingers, Eve suddenly felt a warm tingle rush up her fingers and settle in her chest.

"That is a seeing stone; they are extremely rare," Gwen whispered in an awed voice. "They can only be activated by an elf that has wisdom and the sight. We need to find

Reena." Eve looked up from the stone with a puzzled expression.

"Hold on, a seeing stone? Those are a thing of elvish legend. It's a story Dad used to tell me at bedtime." She looked disbelievingly from the stone to her mother's face and back again. "Right...?"

Gwen gazed upon her beautiful child - in all but blood - knowing what this stone meant and how much it was about to change Eve's life. Whether the change would be for better or worse was not yet clear. One thing was for certain, the only elf who could glean the message from the stone was Reena.

"Let's go find Reena, sweetheart. She will have the answer. Bring the map, maybe she can enlighten us about these other lands as well." Gwen moved toward Eve and put the map and stone back in the wooden box. "Come, the sooner we find her, the sooner you will have answers."

~

REENA, the wise woman gifted with the sight, or so many believed, lived away from other elves. She chose to live deep in the forest, and her home was truly beautiful. She never felt the need to venture far; everything she needed was right on her doorstep. It came as no great surprise to see Gwen and Evangeline approaching that day. The change in the child's eyes only the day before was enough to know that something very special lay in the destiny of young Eve.

~

GWEN RAISED her tea cup to her lips; only Reena could make the perfect rosehip tea. Looking across at the two of them pouring over the map, she couldn't help but feel fearful for her precious child. *She is grown now; I cannot always protect her*, she thought.

"The map shows the five realms of Orea, including our own. You know of the witch's realm, Clear Water Valley. There is also Mieron, the realm of the vampires, Gloria, the realm of the Fae. Tricky folk, the Fae." Reena ran her gnarled fingers over the areas as she named them.

"Now, let me see. Ah yes, and Olia, the realm of the owl riders." Reena finished pointing to the realms on the map and then looked at Eve expectantly.

"There is also this. It was hidden in the lid of the box; Mother says it is a seeing stone. But I thought they were just a legend." Eve finished in a rush. She did not wish to be seen as foolish. Reena took the cool stone from Eve and turned it over in her hands.

It is as I thought. This child is meant for great things. Keeping her thoughts to herself, she looked Eve in the eye and replied, "Yes child, your Mother is quite correct. This is, indeed, a seeing stone. A stone of prophecy."

"Wait… What?" Eve was clearly hearing things. She was sure Reena has just said *a stone of prophecy*. "What does that mean, Reena?" Not sure she really wanted to know the answer, Eve took a step away from the stone, suddenly not as fond of its luster as she had been a moment ago.

"It means, Evangeline, that this stone holds your destiny. However, you do have a choice. I can activate the stone to read the prophecy hidden within, or I can hand it back to you. Only you can choose which path to take; I cannot help you, nor can your mother," Reena explained.

"You must look inside yourself and choose your path. The prophecy is as old as time. We do not know who made the stones… maybe the Goddess herself. The fact remains, this stone was meant for you. A stone of prophecy is guarded by mystical forces, and only the one who is meant to fulfil the prophecy will find the stone, or so the legend reads. Make your choice. Look within yourself; the answer is there for you to find."

This is madness! Eve thought. *Yesterday I was just Eve, a normal girl with a normal family. Today I have luminous eyes, a missing brother, and now this! Why me?* Looking at Reena and her loving mother, she knew what had to be done. The stone had called to her the very first time she had stroked its surface.

"Alright, let's find out what the stone has been keeping secret."

Reena took the stone in her left hand and took Eve's hand in her right. She then began to chant. The sound of it reminded Eve of water flowing over pebbles by the stream; it soothed her. After a few moments, enchanted elvish script appeared on the surface. Reena read it and then relayed the prophecy she had been waiting her whole life to hear.

"Eve, this knowledge was kept from you until eighteen years after your birth. This is your prophecy. Only you can fulfil it."

Reena proceeded to read the prophecy aloud.

"An Elvish girl with changeable eyes will lose her family through the void. Three companions she will travel with. They will be identified by their gems. To get back what was lost, the Aurora stone must return to its home. In no more than a year and four days must this quest be completed, or the realms will be pulled into the void and lost."

COMING SOON

Djinn
The Orea Chronicles Book Two

Sanguisuge
A Vampiric Novella

Under the Candy Moon
Book one of the Dream Walker Series.

ALSO BY ALANA GREIG

THE AURORA STONE: THE OREA CHRONICLES BOOK 1

LOVE YOU IN PIECES: A ZOMBIE ROMANTIC COMDEY.

CO WRITTEN TITLES

ONCE UPON A REALITY. CO WRITTEN WITH ERIN LEE TWICE UPON A REALITY. CO WRITTEN WITH ERIN LEE

THIRD TIME'S A CHARM? CO WRITTEN WITH ERIN LEE

ANTHOLOGIES

THE TROUBLE WITH LOVE IS

FEATURED IN THE CRAZY

ABOUT LOVE ANTHOLOGY

BELLA CHEW CHEW

FEATURED IN THE CRAZY FOOLS ANTHOLOGY

MY MONSTER

FEATURED IN THE INSAINE INSOMNIA ANTHOLOGY

CHOSEN

FEATURED IN A DEADLY WORLD: VAMPIRES IN

PARIS ANTHOLOGY

CAUGHT IN THE ACT

FEATURED IN A DEADLY WORLD: VAMPIRES IN NEW YORK

ANTHOLOGY .

SHORT STORIES

Loving Olivia : A Romance

Whispering Monster : A thriller

Bella Chew chew : A romantic comedy

Lunara 69: 18+ SciFi

ABOUT THE AUTHOR

Alana Greig is a thirty something mother of two and happily married. She lives on the west coast of England and loves to spend time at the beach.

Alana predominantly writes fantasy. *The Aurora Stone* was her debut novel. *Once Upon a Reality* is a collection of short stories based on old classics. Alana co- wrote the books, part of a three-part series, with USA TODAY bestselling author Erin Lee.

Work is also underway for Alana's second novel, *Djinn*, which is based on Princess Winter from *The Aurora Stone*. Finally, Alana is also working on her first Horror/thriller, *WAX*, also due to be released in 2021. When Alana isn't creating new worlds, she loves nothing more than to curl up with a cup of tea and lose herself in someone else's.

For more information about Alana and her books
www.theaccidentalauthor.com
author.alana.greig@outlook.com

facebook.com/TheAlmostBaldGirl84
instagram.com/TheAlmostBaldGirl
amazon.com/Alana-Greig